KV-574-240

Swan Valley Library
Tel: 01322 5·····
Fax: 01322 ·····

Fleetdown Library
Tel/Fax: 01322 225546
Fleetdown Library
Tel/Fax: 01322 225546

R6(H)
R8(E)

13. SEP 07
26. JUL 08
24. JUL 07
28. JUL 08.
17. AUG 07

7 - JUL 2011
19.11.13

Books should be returned or renewed by the
last date stamped above

last
copy

ST CLAIR (JOY)
Love's tangled web

WITHDRAWN

Awarded for excellence
to Arts & Libraries

WDLP3

Kent
County
Council

C152213933

LOVE'S TANGLED WEB

Shelley is in Holland trying to make a new life for herself—a life without men. The yacht her father designed has sunk with a fortune in diamonds on board and the man she thought she loved has jilted her. Then she meets Dirk Joustra, a salvage engineer who hopes to recover the yacht. She falls in love but it is a love that will be tested to the full. Dirk is accused of stealing the diamonds, and Greet, a sad and beautiful Dutchwoman, sets her sights on him.

LOVE'S TANGLED WEB

Love's Tangled Web

by

Joy St. Clair

522|3933

Dales Large Print Books
Long Preston, North Yorkshire,
England.

British Library Cataloguing in Publication Data.

St. Clair, Joy
Love's tangled web.

A catalogue record for this book is
available from the British Library

ISBN 1-85389-602-0 pbk   C152213933

First published in Great Britain by Robert Hale Ltd., 1989

Copyright © 1989 by Joy St. Clair

Published in Large Print February, 1996 by arrangement
with Joy St. Clair.

All rights reserved. No part of this publication may be
reproduced, stored in a retrieval system, or transmitted in any
form or by any means, electronic, mechanical, photocopying,
recording or otherwise, without the prior permission of the
Copyright owner.

Dales Large Print is an imprint of
Library Magna Books Ltd.
Printed and bound in Great Britain by
T.J. Press (Padstow) Ltd., Cornwall, PL28 8RW.

To Charlotte
Because

CHAPTER 1

'You'll have no trouble recognising Joustra,' said the Commandant. 'Friesians are invariably tall and blond.'

As Shelley drove away, she had her doubts. In this land of fair-haired giants one more was bound to be lost in the crowd.

The road into Zandvoort meandered between golden sand dunes and was practically deserted, but in the town the rush-hour traffic was building up as workers hurried home from offices and shops and packed coaches returned holidaymakers to their hotels after a day's sight-seeing in the bulbfields.

The area was typically Dutch, from the neat modern Monopoly board houses to the older buildings featuring picturesque gables and lifting beams, the whole scene providing a sense of history skilfully interwoven with the unembellished lines of the twentieth century.

Shelley loved Holland. It was clean and

honest and practical—like its people.

She stopped the car at the lights while pedestrians with umbrellas surged across. April here was similar to April in England and showers came without warning.

She was first away, expertly handling the large Citroën past the on-coming vehicles and inevitable bicycles. It had been a different story when she had first arrived here, six months earlier, and she had despaired of ever getting the hang of driving on the 'wrong' side of the road. She'd been labouring under a personal crisis then, which hadn't helped. The collapse of her father's business and her broken engagement had undermined her self-confidence, but it was all past history now.

An impatient taxi cut in front of her and, as she was forced to brake, she glanced anxiously at her watch.

She worked as general dogsbody for the Hotel Klokken, a five-star establishment on the outskirts of the seaside town and had been despatched to meet *Mijnheer* Joustra arriving on the five o'clock train from Amsterdam.

'Friesland is in the north and its people are a race apart,' the proprietor had said.

An ex-navy man, known to everyone as the Commandant, with ramrod back and gunmetal hair he was the ideal mine-host and worked hard to maintain a 'happy ship'. 'They're proud of their heritage and it shows in their bearing. You'll see. Better take the Citroën. It'll accommodate *Mijnheer* Joustra's long legs better. Oh yes, he'll have long legs.'

She turned into the station forecourt and parked the car, deciding to let the name of the hotel emblazoned on the side speak for itself, as well as her distinctive uniform of navy and white striped blazer over an orange crystal-pleated dress. If that weren't enough she wore an enamel brooch with the words HOTEL KLOKKEN etched on it, and underneath the name SHELLEY.

She leaned against the bonnet watching the trickle of passengers come through the ticket hall, aware but taking little notice of the interested glances of the men.

The rain persisted and she turned up her collar as the wind tugged her hair. It was waist-length, very dark and thick with a hint of chestnut, deeply waved on the crown and ending in curls, especially profuse around her delicately boned face. Her father considered her beautiful but she couldn't see it. Pretty maybe... Her eyes were strikingly deep blue, like sapphires, her most arresting feature, and even the whites had bluish tints, emphasised by a coating of azure mascara and smoky kohl liner. She had a creamy complexion which tanned easily, but until summer came to Holland, dusted her cheeks with a tawny blusher and applied pink gloss to her small well-defined mouth.

She noticed on the station wall an advertisement for British Rail and experienced a little pang of homesickness for the land of her birth. She indulged it for a moment, having been too busy of late to think of home, a condition which suited her admirably.

Her job here was varied and she enjoyed it enormously, so different from her former employment in the Essex town of Tilbury beside the River Thames. There she had worked as secretary to her father, Frank Pearson, who designed and built sea-going yachts. The firm had been successful but Frank had a dream—to perfect a buoyancy tank which would make the crafts virtually unsinkable. With outside financial backing, he had channelled all his resources into the project—and been ruined as a result.

An old family friend from Holland, Karel van Hoorn, had borrowed the prototype to sail it from London to Amsterdam but the vessel had sunk after striking a log and Karel was presumed drowned, taking with him all Frank's hopes as well as his reputation. Doubts were cast on the worthiness of the new tanks and the backers withdrew their support.

'*Mejuffrouw?*'

A man was surveying her boldly, his cornflower eyes sliding over her face and petite figure with unhurried ease. Tall and slim, he was dressed in the style, if not the quality, of a workman, for his black Kitchener jacket was real leather, his stone-washed jeans were designer-made and she would take a bet on it his checkered lumber shirt bore a 'Turnbull and Asser' label. With his well-travelled canvas holdall, he had to be the Friesian. If more proof were needed his hair was flaxen, dredged with silver, growing just past his ears, with a great sweep across his brow.

His features were angular and over generous, his mouth too wide, his nose too long, his chin too pointed, his brows—a shade darker than his hair—too heavy. His tanned and weather-beaten face lent him the appearance of a marauding warrior of old and a faint scar on one cheek strengthened that aspect. He was probably just the wrong side of thirty and he gave the impression he'd seen it all and done it all, with self-confidence oozing from every relaxed, laid-back pore.

He was easily the most attractive man Shelley had ever seen and her brain went automatically into red alert.

She darted a quick look at his large hands, discovering he wore no ring, but then it was customary for Dutchmen to marry late in life, Dutchwomen to marry early...

She anchored her wayward thoughts and threw her head back to look into his face. His tallness was quite intimidating. She usually wore three-inch heels to combat her lack of height but they were impracticable in the car and her small feet were shod in navy loafers. In the presence of this giant she felt like a pygmy.

'*Mijnheer* Joustra? I'm from the Hotel Klokken,' she said in Dutch, considerably accented.

He grinned lazily and shook her hand. 'You're not a native of Holland, that's for certain. What brings a foreigner to Zandvoort, I wonder. A seasonal job?'

His voice was so low it vibrated like cello strings. His English was good and only the slight blurring of the 'j' and 'w' gave him away.

She continued in Dutch, faltering over the grammar. 'No, I live here, but yes I'm to England.' Darn it, she'd used the wrong preposition! 'I mean from England.'

'Speak English then,' he invited, opening the rear door of the car and slinging his holdall onto the back seat.

As his English was far superior to her Dutch, she acquiesced. 'Very well.' She opened the front passenger door and watched him ease his long legs in before slamming it briskly. She was used to his type. They drifted through the hotel at intervals, on holiday or attending business conventions, free from the inhibitions of their home and office environments, making passes and practising their charm, all to be met with a friendly, but negative response from her.

'It was good of them to send a car,' he said as she climbed into the driver's seat. 'I could have taken a taxi, you know, but they insisted.'

'Yes, it's all part of the service. The proprietor prides himself on it.' She smiled. 'The Hotel Klokken is three miles north of here. How long are you staying?'

'Already wanting to be rid of me?' he enquired teasingly.

'Not at all.' Disconcerted, she crashed the gears. 'Just making conversation.'

'I haven't decided yet how long I shall stay. I've booked a couple of weeks. The rest of my party will be arriving tomorrow.'

'Your wife?' Now why had she asked that?

'I'm not married.' He grinned smugly. 'So now you know.'

'Business or pleasure?' she asked quickly.

'Business. My party consists of my assistant and one other employee. They will arrive by sea.'

The traffic eased and she drove confidently out of town. Aware her companion watched her steadily, she searched her brain for something to say. 'Have you been to Zandvoort before?'

'Not to Zandvoort, although I have visited other towns in the area.'

'You'll like it. It has miles of sandy beaches and quiet dunes.' Her tongue ran away with her. 'Plenty of shops and bistros and fish restaurants and thirty-eight beach pavilions. Plus a casino and an aquarium.' Help, she sounded like a travel brochure!

'It sounds very nice.'

Was he mocking her? 'Then there are the bulbfields. Miles of glasshouses and fields where you can see how flowers can add colour and brightness to spring.'

'Did you read that in Baedeker's?' He chuckled. 'Have you seen the bulbfields yourself?'

'I meant to but I haven't had the time.'

'I thought so. You'd have spoken with more feeling if you had. I've seen them many times.'

The rain ceased but the wind remained strong and the sea looked angry instead of its usual picture postcard calm. High waves rolled in to thunder on the beach and suck back the sand. A couple of bobbing yachts hugged the shore and a few brave swimmers battled against the swell.

'Stop here for a moment, please.' He pointed a finger. 'Pull into that parking space.'

She did as she was told and he climbed out, crunching over the gravelled promenade overlooking the straight beach below with its cafes and sunbathing stations, all closed so early in the season.

She stayed where she was and gazed out over the stretch of water where all her father's dreams had foundered. It was here, six miles out, that Karel van Hoorn had come to grief in the *Angela Rose*—named after Shelley's late mother—and it had sunk in fifty feet of water.

She shivered and looked away. Catching sight of her windswept reflection in the mirror she turned her collar down, revealing her name brooch, and tried to smooth her hair into some sort of order.

Joustra returned and stared deliberately down at her. 'Your hair is beautiful.'

She had a desire to cut him down to size, but suppressed it. *'Dankjewel.'*

'And thank you for stopping.' He got in and glanced at her brooch. 'Miss?'

She didn't know if he was asking her name or her married status. She nodded and said 'Pearson,' answering both questions.

He shrugged eloquently, a truly continental gesture. 'I thought English girls married young. What are you? Twenty-one?'

'Twenty-two, if it's any of your business.'

'Sorry.'

'No, I'm sorry.' She was blithely un-repentant. 'I'm not supposed to be cheeky to the guests.'

He watched her shrewdly then took a notepad and pen from his jacket pocket and scribbled a few notes, speaking to her out of the corner of his mouth. 'Your emotional hang-ups are showing, Miss Pearson. Some guy let you down?'

Despite the harshness of the remark, he sounded sympathetic. She clamped her lips together hard. Pity was the last thing she wanted. She was thoroughly disoriented by now and had to make a seven-point turn to get them back on the road.

'Do you want me to drive?' he offered.

'Certainly not!' She pressed her foot hard on the accelerator and the car shot forward in a series of jerks before stalling.

She heard him laugh, a deep throaty sound. His perception was maddening, she thought as she brought the car under control. Some guy indeed!

She'd been engaged to Ryder Channing, her father's right-hand man and at first had thought the collapse of the firm was to blame for putting a strain on their relationship. But it was worse than that—much worse.

She pictured him, the dream-filled quality of his wide-set topaz eyes, the laughter that lurked in his expression, the determined curving mouth which had the power to move her to paradise—or to purgatory, the cloud of dark hair which would not be tamed. When she was in his arms nothing else had mattered. She had loved everything about him, from his quick brain to his easy loping walk. Besides being a genius with paperwork, he was an all-round athlete, excelling in water sports, which had made him invaluable to Frank Pearson.

Why was she thinking about all this now? She had promised never to pick over the bones again. Try as she might she could not get off the carousel of memories and the more she struggled the faster it revolved through her mind.

Ryder had certainly known how to make a girl feel special. Flowers would arrive on the flimsiest of pretexes. One day he would present her with an expensive perfume, the next a packet of Smarties. Her bedroom shelf had been filled with shells he'd brought up from the ocean floor. Once a taxi delivered a valentine card four feet high by three feet wide. She had known him for four years and not visualised life without him...

'Stop!' It was the Friesian yelling in her ear.

She braked hard, thankful for seatbelts. 'I thought you were going through that red light.'

'Sorry.' What was the matter with her?

They got the green and she put her mind to the matter in hand.

'I must have touched a raw nerve,' he commented.

She lifted her chin defiantly but admitted the betrayal still hurt, still clung like scent to an article long since discarded. 'Not at all, Mr Joustra.'

'Do drop the mister.' He made another note on the pad. 'My first name is Diederik, but my friends call me Dirk.' He eyed the brooch again. 'And you're Shelley, I see, a beautiful name for a beautiful girl.'

She squirmed at the cliché but was on familiar ground now. Passes she could handle. *Dankjewel.*

'It's best to get down to first names if we're going to see a lot of each other.'

She deliberately misunderstood. 'I don't think we'll be seeing a lot of each other. I'm a skivvy, not a waitress or a chambermaid. You won't be seeing me.'

He turned down the corners of his mouth. 'But you're having dinner with me this evening, aren't you?'

'Sorry. I have to work.'

'I thought keeping the guests happy was part of it.' He chewed the pen and jotted down a set of figures.

She had been flirted with before, many times, but never so offhandedly and it irritated her. 'May I remind you I'm not one of the facilities of the hotel.' She wondered why she was reacting so positively to his advances, but sensed a certain amount of attraction between them that could not be denied. It had been a long time since she had felt such a need to be on her guard.

He put the notepad away. 'Do you live in?'

'No.' They had reached a cluster of bungalows opposite the hotel drive. 'I live over there with my godmother.'

She had no intention of explaining how she, an English girl, came to be living in Holland. Besides being none of his business, the whole story was too sensitive and, like everything else, dated back to the sinking of the *Angela Rose.*

Within weeks of the disaster her father had departed for Saudi Arabia to work on a pipeline in order to raise enough cash to repay his creditors and she had been left high and dry, with no job and no prospects. And no fiancé.

Karel Van Hoorn had been a respected citizen of Zandvoort and Shelley dutifully attended his memorial service. At the reception afterwards, Karel's British-born widow had sensed Shelley's desperation and invited her to come to live with her in Holland.

Shelley had gratefully accepted even though she felt guilty about the death of Karel, apparently due indirectly to her father's incompetence. But Lorraine van Hoorn was a lonely woman and insisted she would be glad of her goddaughter's company. Lorraine had provided a comfortable home but Shelley soon tired of lazing around all day brooding over Ryder's treachery. So she had taken the job at the Hotel Klokken which now loomed ahead, approached by a sweeping drive thickly lined with rhododendron and magnolia trees.

'Here we are then.' She brought the car

to a halt before the ancient building, as big as a town hall, with bell gables, iron balconies and a large fifteenth-century gilt clock after which it was named.

She waited while Dirk retrieved his holdall from the rear seat, then accompanied him to the reception desk where the proprietor was waiting to extend his hospitality.

The Commandant ran his eyes over the Friesian and shot an 'I told you so' glance at Shelley. 'I trust you had a pleasant journey, *Mijnheer* Joustra, and the car was to your liking.'

'Very pleasant,' Dirk replied with conventional Dutch courtesy. 'The car was comfortable and its driver delightful.' To Shelley he murmured, 'I particularly liked the seven-point turn—and the emergency stop.'

She grinned and went along the corridor to the lounge to look for her godmother, who always came over for an aperitif at this hour of the day.

Lorraine van Hoorn sat alone in the window, sipping a *bessen-jenever*. She was a tall, willowy woman, formerly a top model in London, now well-known locally as a sculptress. Although she was in her

24

early fifties, her features still retained the classic alabaster beauty which had gazed so radiantly from a thousand magazine covers. An emerald suit complemented her auburn hair, tinged with grey streaks which she made no attempt to disguise, and her flawless make-up enhanced her pale skin and high cheekbones.

'Hello dear, been busy?' she asked as Shelley, a glass of tonic water in her hand, dropped into a wicker chair beside her.

'I had to pick up a guest from the station.'

'You look preoccupied. Trouble?'

'Nothing I couldn't handle.' Shelley smiled at the woman she had known and loved all her life.

Lorraine and Shelley's father had grown up together and been expected to marry. But each had found happiness with another partner. Frank Pearson had married Lorraine's colleague, Angela, and Lorraine had wed Karel van Hoorn. Even though they lived in different countries the families had kept in close contact.

'You've gone very quiet,' Lorraine was saying. 'I hope you're not brooding again. I thought this job would keep you too busy to dwell on the past and help you meet

25

new friends. You're too young to have locked your heart away in a lavender-scented drawer.'

Before Shelley could reply there was a movement in the doorway and everyone in the room looked up as Lorraine's daughter, Greet Busieau, made her entrance.

She was certainly a beauty and her clothes fairly shrieked her femininity, her leopard-skin pants fitting like a second skin, her high breasts thrusting against an expensive silk shirt. She had inherited her mother's fine bone structure and her hair was a glorious ginger, piled high on her head with a halo of tendrils framing her face. Her dove-coloured eyes smouldered with an awareness of the admiring glances she was receiving, but her small pouting mouth conferred an impression of discontentment. She was four years older than Shelley and lived in the south of France. With a failed marriage to a wealthy Belgian industrialist behind her and a generous divorce settlement in the bank, she had turned up two weeks ago to stay at the bungalow.

For all Greet's style and beauty, Shelley couldn't help but feel sorry for the way things had developed for this restless young woman who had all her life dwelt unconsciously in the shadow of her elegant mother.

Greet fetched a *Parfait Amour* from the bar and came over to join them, addressing Shelley in clipped English. 'Who was that Adonis you just brought in? I saw you from the window of the bungalow...'

'And hurried over to stake your claim,' Shelley finished. 'Diederik Joustra—a Friesian.'

'Obviously!' Greet dug one slender heel into the thick carpet and crossed her endless legs. 'But you saw him first.'

'Be my guest.' Out of the corner of her eye Shelley saw Dirk framed in the doorway.

Greet saw him too and licked her lips like a gourmet contemplating the menu. 'I'll remember you said that.'

Their gentle sparring was reminiscent of the innocent rivalry of their youth when the girls had shared their summer holidays in each other's countries.

Dirk's eyes swept the gathering and he made an unerring line for the three women. He had changed into a shaggy white turtle-neck sweater which accented his tanned face and neck. He was certainly

27

an attractive man and Shelley's wasn't the only female head that turned in his direction.

He towered above her, about to speak, but Greet cut in quickly, 'I do hope you're going to introduce us to your friend, Shelley.'

'Lorraine, Greet, this is Mr Joustra. My godmother, Mrs van Hoorn and her daughter, *Mrs* Busieau.' For some reason she put particular emphasis on Greet's title.

It made no difference for Greet qualified. 'Divorced. Adultery. His.'

'Greet!' Lorraine, who had absorbed the Dutch penchant for decorum, was aghast at her daughter's outspokenness. 'Really!'

They shook hands all round and Dirk called to the waiter to bring him a pils beer. It arrived and he seated himself beside Shelley.

'Mrs van Hoorn?' he asked. 'You wouldn't be Karel's widow by any chance?'

'Why yes.' Lorraine's face lit up and she leaned forward eagerly, always pleased to meet someone who had been acquainted with her husband. 'You knew him?'

'Not directly. I knew of him.' Dirk took

a gulp from his glass. 'I never expected to meet you here.'

'But I live here,' said Lorraine, mystified. 'Karel and I lived all our married lives in a bungalow across the road.'

'Yes, I know. However I assumed you would have moved away after his death, gone back to England possibly. You are English?'

'Yes, but I've lived in Holland for thirty years and this is my home,' she protested. 'All my memories are here.'

Greet expressed a sigh of annoyance with the way her mother was monopolising Dirk's attention. 'What brings you here, Mr Joustra? A holiday?'

'Hardly. I'm the director of Joustra Salvage.' He watched Lorraine closely. 'You've probably heard of us.'

She stiffened and the colour drained from her face. 'Salvage? You mean... Oh no!'

Shelley gazed from one to the other of them wondering what was the matter with Lorraine, who was usually so composed, and why that seemingly innocent word had caused her to look so troubled.

'Lorraine, what is it?' she asked sharply. 'You look as if you've seen a ghost.'

'A ghost?' Lorraine's voice was strained, barely audible. 'Yes.' She blinked rapidly then her lips compressed into a tight line of censure. 'It's quite simple, Shelley. Mr Joustra is here to salvage the *Angela Rose.*' She challenged him. 'Am I right?'

He nodded and said evenly, 'I'm going to try.'

Shelley felt her scalp tingle. After all these months someone was going to make another attempt to find the yacht!

She frowned. 'But the insurance firm searched twenty square miles of the area and had no luck.'

'If it's there I'll find it,' he declared confidently. 'And the diamonds too!'

CHAPTER 2

Time seemed to stand still.

The memories which had been coming back in bits and pieces all afternoon erupted and Shelley's thoughts returned to that fateful day, last October, when Karel van Hoorn had called at her father's boatyard in Tilbury to borrow the *Angela*

Rose because his own craft had broken down just after leaving Tower Bridge.

Karel was a courier for a firm of Dutch diamond merchants and had been engaged to transport a million pounds' worth of uncut diamonds from Hatton Gardens in London to Amsterdam. He was a competent sailor and had made the trip single-handed many times before. It was considered the safest method of moving such a valuable haul. Who would think a yacht would contain such a treasure? When he had asked to sail the forty-foot prototype with the controversial buoyancy tanks, Frank Pearson had been delighted, seeing it as an independent test for his 'baby'.

Frank had accompanied Karel through Customs and seen the diamonds safely transferred to a water-tight compartment on the *Angela Rose,* then kept in radio contact with the Dutchman throughout the hundred-and-fifty-mile journey to Holland, which was expected to take twenty-four hours.

However, just six miles west of Zandvoort, Karel had radioed a garbled message saying he had hit a log and the yacht was sinking fast, the special tanks seemingly having no effect.

Other shipping, too far away to help, had reported seeing distress flares, but by the time they arrived on the scene, the *Angela Rose* had disappeared. After an extensive search, Karel had been presumed drowned in fifty feet of water, and the discovery of the mast on the beach the following morning seemed to confirm this.

The whole terrible tragedy had brought Shelley her share of misery, for it was directly due to the sinking that she had been deserted by Ryder.

It was clear in retrospect that Ryder had proposed to her, the boss's daughter, to further his career. He was an ambitious man. Orphaned at an early age, brought up by indifferent foster parents, his one aim was to succeed. After Frank was ruined and there was no career left with Pearson Marine, Ryder had told her it was all over between them.

At first she had refused to believe it. After all his promises, the intimacy they had shared, how could he tell her he had stopped loving her?

Yet there was a limit to the length to which she could deceive herself. She had been taken in by a handsome face and a clever tongue.

All too late she had discovered what kind of man Ryder Channing was. Not dreams in his eyes but calculations, not determination on his lips, but ruthlessness. The bitter truth was that she had given her heart to a perfect stranger—and foolishly thought she held his.

It was then she had needed the comfort of her mother who had died of influenza eight years earlier. Her father had been too wrapped up in his own problems to notice the pounding Shelley had taken. So she had drifted, in a kind of limbo, rapidly losing confidence in herself as a woman.

When she finally surfaced from that wasteland of despair she had been surprised to find how resilient she had become, how wary of making the same mistake again.

Oh yes, she had a great deal of interest in what Dirk Joustra was proposing to do.

Lorraine broke the silence at last. 'It was a very harrowing experience.' Her eyes clouded with anguish. 'Must you revive the matter?'

'Salvage is my business,' said Dirk. 'I've signed a contract with the insurance company to go fifty-fifty on anything I find. I owe it to my shareholders to do my utmost to recover the diamonds.'

'What if you find nothing?' Lorraine twirled the stem of her glass. 'What if the yacht is too deep? The insurance company were very thorough and they drew a blank.'

'Forgive me if I sound boastful,' said Dirk, 'but in my opinion their divers gave up too soon. I wasn't available at the time so they were forced to opt for second best. If I can't find the yacht then no-one can. Until I've tried I won't know.' His eyes grew hooded. 'Frankly, Mrs van Hoorn, I thought you'd be pleased to have the matter cleared up once and for all, to know for certain how your husband met his death.'

'Well, I'm not.' She stared back. 'It was a terrible shock at the time and I don't relish a repeat performance. Aspersions were cast on Karel's character—and mine too. Can you imagine what it was like, having the bungalow searched? Policemen tramping about, sifting through my possessions, tapping walls, digging up the garden? In the end it was agreed that everything was as it appeared. Now you'll stir it all up again and people who have forgotten will point the accusing finger again.'

'Not if I find the yacht and prove

everything is as it appeared,' reasoned Dirk. He turned to Shelley. 'And what do you think?'

For a moment she was torn between loyalty to her godmother and a desire for the truth. 'I think it might be best to leave things as they are. The suspicions made Lorraine ill. I wouldn't like her to go through all that again.'

'You can't be serious,' he persisted. 'Don't you want to know whether or not your father's tanks were faulty?'

She gasped. 'How did you know who I was?'

'I guessed. Your name. The fact that Mrs van Hoorn is your godmother. It all adds up to your being Frank Pearson's daughter.' He leaned towards her urgently. 'Well, don't you want to know...one way or the other?'

She bit her lip in consternation. She didn't want to side with Dirk against Lorraine, who had been like a second mother to her, and yet she was curious to know what had caused the yacht to sink. At the same time she couldn't face the thought that her father might after all be proved to have invented a worthless tank, an invention that had resulted in a man's death. And no ordinary man—the husband of a lifelong friend.

Dirk was reading her mind. 'You want the yacht found—but only if it exonerates your father. Is that it?'

She glared at him as the colour raced to her cheeks, and opened her mouth to deny it, but Lorraine intervened.

'Mr Joustra, that yacht is my husband's grave. It must not be disturbed. You know the law.'

'That law only applies to vessels sunk during wartime,' he replied scathingly.

'How callous you sound! Have you no ethics?'

'A million pounds' worth of diamonds make ethics expensive,' he intoned dryly. 'My assistant is bringing a small salvage vessel to Zandvoort tomorrow. We would have started sooner but have been engaged all year on a wreck off the Spanish coast. As soon as they arrive we will start operations. I'm afraid there's nothing you can do about it, Mrs van Hoorn.'

'No?' She stood up abruptly. 'We'll see about that, I have many friends in local government circles.'

He shrugged negligently. 'Do your worst.'

Shelley rose also, but Dirk caught her wrist in a loose grip. 'You still haven't answered my question.'

She hesitated. 'I...go along with my godmother. I think it's despicable to disturb Karel's grave.'

'Come off it!' he said harshly. 'You're chicken!'

She pulled her hand away.

Greet laughed. 'Save your breath, Mr Joustra. You'll never convince these two you're not a ghoul.'

He threw her a grateful smile, then cocked an eyebrow at Shelley. 'What about dinner tonight?'

'I told you. I'm working.'

Greet's voice oozed with sensuality. 'I'm available for dinner.'

As Shelley weaved between the little tables in Lorraine's wake, a backward glance showed Greet leaning towards Dirk and the two of them laughing together. She marched out of the hotel wondering why the cameo scene she had witnessed caused her such a stab of resentment.

'Oh, Shelley,' sighed Lorraine as they crossed the road to the bungalow nestling in a beech spinney beside the dunes.

'The wretched business will start all over again.'

'Don't upset yourself, dear. I think it highly unlikely Dirk will locate the yacht, despite his egocentric talk. The divers engaged by the insurance company were thorough, whatever he says. And six months have passed since then. It's probably broken up by now...' She saw Lorraine's stricken expression and stopped. 'Don't worry.'

The bungalow was an attractive L-shaped building. Its white walls were criss-crossed with leafy trellises and hanging in every window was a *sier horretje*—a little wire screen covered with lace on which was embroidered a windmill motif. Lorraine unlocked the door. 'I can't help worrying. Without a body nothing is conclusive. You don't suppose...?'

Shelley looked pityingly into the tragic face. What could she say to offer some comfort? Insist that Karel was dead? That would be too brutal. But to suggest he was alive, in hiding, with the diamonds...! Shelley could not voice such a thought, even though it must have crossed everyone's mind, including Lorraine's.

Shelley was spared the ordeal of having

to reply as Lorraine muttered, 'I've heard about Joustra Salvage. Everybody has. They're not as esteemed as that man would have us believe. They're not above under-handed dealings. Why, I recall a court case they were involved in.'

Shelley was intrigued. 'Go on!'

'Oh, I can't remember the details. But there was a big *brouhaha* over some banknotes missing from a tanker they towed in. One of the partners of Joustra Salvage took the blame and was sent to prison. Not Joustra, he was too clever. I don't trust him. He's ruthless.'

They entered the wide hall cluttered, Dutch fashion, with occasional furniture.

The aroma of beef stew tempted Shelley into the Delft-tiled kitchen where an earthenware saucepan stood on a large ceramic stove. She had removed the saucepan lid and taken up a wooden spoon when she realised Lorraine was not behind her.

She retraced her steps and saw her godmother in the hall, unlocking the door at the end. Shelley followed inquisitively.

It was only the second time since his death she had seen the interior of Karel's study for it had been turned into a shrine and the door was kept locked, the key suspended on a chain around Lorraine's neck.

All his things were here as he had left them. There were photographs and trophies for sailing, plus his pipe-rack and fishing-rod. His jacket hung over a chair, as if he had just popped out and would be back any moment.

Shelley shivered involuntarily.

In pride of place in the bow window was a bust of Karel, lovingly sculptured by Lorraine, which captured the man's sad expression. He had walked with a slight limp—the result of a motoring accident—and been a quiet, morose person, the perfect foil for his vivacious red-haired wife.

'Oh Shelley!' Lorraine's fingers caressed the marble contours of his face. 'I can feel him near me.'

'Lorraine, come away please.' Shelley forced a bright tone. 'Dinner smells good...'

They heard the front door slam and footsteps tread the hall.

Another shiver assailed Shelley. But it was not the ghost of Karel. Only Greet. The Dutchwoman threw her bag on the hall table and came to investigate the open door.

'Mother! What are you doing in this room? You know how it upsets you.'

'On the contrary, it calms me.' Lorraine ushered Shelley out and locked the door again.

Greet removed the pins from her hair and fluffed it into a glorious ginger haze. 'You should get rid of all that junk in there. It's too macabre. Give it away to *Zak van Max* or the *Legerdes Heils.*' She flung Shelley a rapid translation. 'Oxfam and the Salvation Army.'

Lorraine pretended she hadn't heard and hastened away to see to the dinner.

Greet surveyed Shelley from dreamy grey eyes. 'Dirk's an exciting man. I might amuse myself with him for a day or two. That is, if you have no objections.'

Shelley tossed her dark head. 'Help yourself.'

Shelley returned to the hotel to work that evening and was taking her turn at the reception desk when the internal phone rang. It was Dirk, asking for a cup of hot chocolate to be brought to his suite. He spoke in Dutch but easily switched to

English when he realised it was her.

'I'll see the porter brings it straight away.'

'Won't you bring it yourself?' His tone was intimate and teasing and she pictured the curving of his lips.

'Sorry, I can't leave the desk,' she lied, annoyed to find herself coyly twisting her pencil into her hair.

'I bet you could if you tried.'

'Sorry,' she repeated and rang off.

She beckoned to Popken, the artful old porter who went to great lengths to dodge his share of the work. At once he put on a pained expression and rubbed his calf. He had been using his old war wound as an excuse the past couple of days and Shelley knew it would be futile asking him to do anything. She told him to watch the desk and went to the kitchen for the chocolate.

Carrying it carefully on a tray she took the lift to the fourth floor and trudged the thick carpets to tap smartly on the door of Dirk's suite.

'*Kom binnen,*' he called, plainly expecting the porter.

She opened the door a fraction and, hearing the buzz of an electric shaver somewhere out of sight, swiftly crossed the sitting-room to deposit the tray on a low table. The wide sliding doors leading to the bedroom were open and she glimpsed clothes scattered carelessly over the bed.

She turned to make her getaway, but before she reached the door Dirk stepped from the bathroom and barred her way.

'Don't run away.'

There was the scent of a musky cologne clinging to him and his locks were damp from the shower. He wore a black karate-style robe which swung open to reveal long legs covered with shaggy gold hair.

Shelley felt a half-forgotten tingling in the pit of her stomach.

'Changed your mind about bringing the drink? Decided you wanted to see me after all?'

'No-one else was available.'

'Won't you join me? I'll send down for another chocolate.'

'No thanks.'

He still blocked her way and she saw the playful glint in his cornflower eyes. There were little silver flecks in them she hadn't noticed before.

'I must go.'

'I expect you'll be off duty soon,' he

mused. 'Then it's away to meet the boy-friend... Or the fiancé perhaps. What does he think of your working all evening?'

'I have no boy-friend...' She stopped self-consciously. It was none of his business.

'You're very jittery,' he observed. 'You've been working too hard. Stay and relax a little.'

'No thank you.'

He shook his head sadly. 'It's very much as I thought.'

Needlessly straightening her jacket, she asked, 'What's that supposed to mean?'

'That guy really exists. The one who let you down so badly. He's not a figment of my imagination after all.' He rubbed his smooth jaw thoughtfully. 'There's only one way to get over a broken romance.'

'Oh yes?' She was sure she shouldn't have asked. His reply was bound to be fatuous.

He grinned. 'Find someone else.'

A laugh erupted inside her. 'Thanks. I'll think about it.' She pivoted on her heel and made what she hoped was a dignified exit.

The next morning Shelley was watering the plants on the hotel terrace when Greet arrived. Dressed in a baggy green cashmere sweater and black culottes and wearing her hair in two schoolgirl bunches, she had succeeded in looking sophisticated and innocent at the same time.

'What brings you here this early?' asked Shelley. 'You don't usually get up before eleven. Oh, I get it, you're stalking your prey.'

Greet grinned wryly. 'Well, it's done me no good. The Commandant says Dirk's hired a van and driven into Zandvoort to meet the salvage vessel.' With an elegant patent leather shoe she kicked at a tuft of grass growing between the flagstones.

She was like a cat on heat, thought Shelley. Poor Greet. Before her marriage she had also been a model and, although successful in her own way, simply hadn't been in Lorraine's class. People had inevitably compared them and, while Greet did not resent her mother's prestige, the constant reminder of it made her restless—and vulnerable.

'Have you seen him this morning?' Greet's grey eyes were as wide as a child's.

'No, he must have been up and away before I arrived.' Shelley pulled a face.

'And that suits me fine.'

'Why? Don't you like him? What's he done?'

'Nothing. It's just that he...bothers me.'

'Is that why you're blushing like a teenager?'

The two women exchanged grins, understanding one another perfectly. They had spent their childhood holidays together in England and Holland and had always enjoyed a friendly argument. Shelley was Lorraine's godchild and Greet was Frank's. It was the closest to a sister either of them had.

Greet, four years older, had always seemed so grown-up and worldlywise to Shelley. The escapades she had led them into! And the excuses Shelley had invented to get the older girl out of trouble! Like the time they had gone to summer camp in Cornwall and Greet had crept out at midnight to indulge in nude bathing... Like the time, in Amsterdam, when Greet had been caught underage in a canalside bar...

'What made you come back to stay with your mother? Zandvoort in April isn't exactly life in the fast lane.'

'A good question.' Greet sighed. 'But

lately I've felt as if I'm drifting. Going from one fashionable resort to the next can be expensive. Frankly I'm running out of money and wanted a break before going after husband Number Two!'

Shelley was shocked but before she could reply saw her employer beckoning her. 'Duty calls. See you later.'

'Mr Joustra will be back soon,' said the Commandant. 'His assistant's staying here. The other man has relatives over in Haarlem and will be staying with them. I want you to see that Popken's available to unload the luggage. He's been skulking off these past few days...'

It was late afternoon before the hired van arrived, by which time Popken had done a disappearing act. She found him having a crafty smoke in the rear courtyard and hustled him, complaining, to the front of the hotel.

As they rounded the corner Dirk alighted from the van. At the same time the back doors opened and a giant of a man, dressed in lumber jacket and jeans, eased himself out.

'Shelley, this is Henk,' Dirk said.

'Hi!' she grinned, thinking that with hands like hams and legs like tree trunks,

Hunk might be a better name.

She grabbed a suitcase from the back of the van as the front passenger door opened and out stepped a tall slim man with an untameable cloud of dark brown hair.

There was something familiar about his bearing and Shelley trembled. As he turned to face her, she froze.

Dirk's voice came to her as if from a distance. 'And this is my assistant, Ryder Channing.'

CHAPTER 3

'Ryder!' White-faced, Shelley swayed on her legs and thought she was going to faint. She'd often speculated how she would react if she met Ryder again. She'd even rehearsed what she would say. Something icily polite, or brilliantly sarcastic. Or, she might cut him dead and walk on by. But now the moment of truth was here and she did none of those things. She merely stood there gaping while a medley of thoughts spun in her brain.

'Shelley?' He looked as stunned as she. 'I can't believe it.' He moved forward with the grace of a jungle cat, topaz eyes concerned. 'Are you all right?'

She knew Dirk watched her and tried to remain calm, not break down here in front of everyone.

Ryder grasped her hand. 'You look terrific. You haven't changed a bit. Still as pretty as ever.'

Her gaze took stock of his smart beige suit and crisp coffee-coloured shirt. He still appeared incredibly handsome and the tiny crinkles beside his eyes tugged at her emotions, while his smooth tones oozed platitudes.

She listened without absorbing one word, letting the sound of his voice wash over her, the deep laugh-filled voice that had haunted her dreams.

'I can't get over it.' He turned to Dirk. 'Shelley and I go way back.'

'Really.' Dirk's tone was dry as dust.

Ryder swung back to her. 'What are you doing here?'

A shaft of sunlight played on his hair, highlighting the nut-brown sheen and tipping the curls with caramel.

'I...live here with my godmother, Lorraine van Hoorn.' Her voice sounded strange to her ears.

He snapped his fingers. 'Ah yes, I remember, you had friends in Zandvoort. But it never entered my head you'd be here. I thought you'd gone to Saudi Arabia with Frank.'

He was chatting away as if nothing had happened and yet there was an underlying edginess about him and she observed the cautious glances he darted at Dirk as he spoke. She couldn't even guess how he had acquired the job as Dirk's assistant.

'How is Frank, by the way?' Ryder asked.

'Well enough.' She felt as if she'd been kicked hard in the solar plexus and wanted to be alone to think and pull herself together.

She took a firmer grip on the suitcase she had picked up, but he wrestled it from her hand and walked beside her up the hotel steps. 'You must be wondering what I'm doing here. I've been working for Joustra Salvage since I left Pearson Marine.' He added with a touch of pride, 'I'm a bloody good diver and a wizard with the ledgers. In fact I'm just the man Joustra needs. He's made me a junior partner in the firm.'

In the foyer he set the case down and

took her hand again. 'It's good to see you, Shelley, after so long.'

She saw Dirk come through the doors and stare at them grimly, his brows meeting in disapproval.

She pulled her hand away and turned to go.

'I'll see you later,' called Ryder.

Shelley's mind was a hotch-potch of thoughts as she let herself out of the back door and leaned crazily against the fence. How could he walk in here and talk so tritely? Did he think he was going to pick up the pieces where he'd left them? And if so, would she have the strength of mind to refuse him? She still trembled from the touch of his hand.

She braced her shoulders. The world had taken a number of turns since she had loved him. She was a survivor, someone who had gone to hell and back and was still standing, wiser and more resilient. Wasn't she?

Later that evening she was pushing a trolley, loaded with glasses, along the rose-lit corridor in the direction of the ballroom, from whence came the lilting strains of a Viennese waltz, when she heard someone call to her from a darkened recess.

She jumped as Ryder stepped into the light. 'Shelley!'

'Excuse me, I'm busy...' She faltered.

His liquid eyes were clear as crystal with an openness that could strip bare the unsuspecting soul and they glowed incandescently under the muted lamps. 'Shelley, my dear, I was concerned about you after we broke off our engagement.'

She was shaking like an aspen leaf and disconcerted to see the lost look that befell his expression.

'Please don't,' she croaked.

'I hurt you badly,' he went on broodingly, 'But I felt the pain, too, you know.'

Then why didn't you come back to me, she thought bitterly, why didn't you make things right again? She said, 'Water under the bridge.'

He touched her shoulder. 'It was only after we'd parted that I realised how it must have looked.'

The words dropped like stones into a lake as she watched the emotions crossing his features—guilt, regret, remorse. Were any of them genuine? What a fool she'd been!

'Tell me you forgive me.'

She said, quickly, 'Yes, Ryder, I forgive you,' amazed to discover it was true.

'Thank you, my dear.' He smiled his charismatic smile but it failed to move her. 'You can't know the torment I've been through.'

What about my torment, she thought? All that suffering in the sleepless nights? As she listened to the glib phrases tripping from his honeyed tongue, she grew calm, surprised she could look at him so objectively. She'd had six months to get him out of her system and knew without a shadow of a doubt he no longer held any attraction for her. She was cured of Ryder once and for all. Over him!

Relief poured over her in a healing stream. She would never be so stupid again. She had learned her lesson—the hard way.

'Shelley,' he said urgently. 'Let's get together for a discreet drink, shall we? Soon.'

She frowned at his choice of adjective. Discreet? What was he trying to hide?

'I don't deserve it,' he murmured silkily, 'But I want to explain. Will you meet me later in the Noordzee bar!'

It was an intimate little bar in the cellar.

In total control of her emotions now she saw no reason to refuse. It certainly wouldn't get him anywhere. 'Yes, yes,' she said impatiently. 'But I have to work right now.'

'A little kiss then, for old time's sake?' His hand was touching her face, smoothing her soft skin and she was astonished to find the action irritated her. She averted her head and his lips feathered her cheek.

Someone cleared his throat nearby, a loud forced noise, and she felt Ryder's nervous start.

'I was looking for you, Ryder,' said Dirk, his voice low and ominous, his eyes savagely raking the two of them as he lounged against the newel post at the foot of the stairs. 'I wanted to go over some calculations with you, but if you're busy...'

A guilty stain suffused Ryder's face. He reminded Shelley of a schoolboy caught smoking behind the bike shed.

'Go along to the reading-room and I'll join you in a moment.' Dirk's tone was authoritative, strengthening the image of a headmaster ordering a boy to wait outside his door.

Ryder needed no second bidding and

Shelley watched his lean figure stride away along the corridor.

She had an idea Dirk was going to start ordering her about too. 'Excuse me.' She tried to push past him but he stood before her like a brick wall, his hand on her arm.

'Let me go, please. I'm working.'

'Now, look here,' he grated out. 'I don't know what happened between you and Ryder in the past, but it's over!'

She was unable to credit what she had heard. 'How dare you!' She winced as his fingers dug tighter into her wrist. 'What's it to do with you? Mind your own business!'

'It's over!' he repeated, his eyes two hard pebbles boring into her.

She shook her arm in a valiant effort to be free of him, but his fingers were like steel clamps. 'Who do you think you are? I shall talk with whom I please. Who gave you the right to interfere? Just keep out of my life!'

He let her go but his tall frame continued to block her way.

Slowly he ran his gaze over her face and figure and his mouth quirked insolently. 'I'm not a fool. He's the one. The guy who soured your life. Well, just you keep away from him. Understand?'

She swallowed a primitive urge to slap his arrogant face and clamped her lips together in a mutinous line. Nothing would induce her to disclose that her feelings for Ryder were dead. Dirk was behaving impertinently and didn't deserve such consideration. She rubbed her bruised wrist and met his eyes steadily.

His hands shot out again, like mechanical grabs. He gave her shoulders a little shake. 'Understand?'

'No, I don't.' Her eyes gleamed with dislike. 'I shall speak to him if I want to. I shall kiss him if I want to. I shall have a mad torrid affair with him...'

'No, you won't!' Dirk bit out each word fiercely, his face a mask of fury. 'He's a married man now and you'll keep away from him.'

'Married?' She felt a rapid pulse in her throat, threatening to choke her. Her senses swam, blurred, merged. The world reeled about her. This was something she hadn't bargained for and, despite her brave conviction that she was over Ryder, it hurt. Hurt like hell! The minutes ticked by and she gulped for oxygen, willing her nerves to steady.

Somewhere a door slammed and she flinched, pulling her eyes away from Dirk's condemning glance. Slowly she regained her equilibrium and let out a deep sigh.

Dirk's features hardened to a hawklike expression, cold and menacing. 'He's married to my sister, Tilda.' He shoved her away. 'So keep your greedy little hands off!'

Somehow she got through the rest of the evening. Hours later she dragged herself home and crawled into bed, her brain still wrestling with uncontrollable thoughts.

So Ryder was running true to form. From the way he had spoken—suggesting a discreet *tête-à-tête*—it was plain his marriage vows were no more binding than his engagement promise had been. He had married Dirk's sister to worm his way into Joustra Salvage, just as he had used Shelley to curry favour with Frank Pearson.

She tried to imagine the kind of woman Tilda was. A carbon copy of herself perhaps? If so then she was to be pitied. And yet... Shelley experienced a pang of jealousy too for the girl who had succeeded where she had failed.

She was awakened by a finger of weak sunshine that prised a gap in the curtain to stab at her eyes.

A knock on the door heralded Lorraine with breakfast on a tray—coffee, bread, little pats of butter and *hagelslag*.

'I thought I'd spoil you, dear. You looked ghastly when you arrived home last night. What happened?'

'Ryder is here.' Shelley balanced the tray on her knees. 'In Zandvoort.'

'Ryder? But how...what...?'

Shelley picked up the delicate bone china cup and sipped the aromatic black coffee. 'He's Dirk's assistant.'

'I see.' Lorraine perched on the edge of the bed. 'And how do you feel about seeing him again?'

'I don't feel anything.' Shelley sprinkled a spoonful of the chocolate vermicelli onto a thick slice of bread and butter. 'I get the impression he's the same old Ryder.' She munched thoughtfully. 'But I'm not the same old Shelley.'

'No I don't think you are.' Lorraine's fingers pleated the hem of the coverlet. 'Love is strange. It does funny things to woman. I once thought I loved your father...'

Shelley knew the story by heart but guessed Lorraine needed to talk. 'Go on!'

'We were young, two bare-limbed children running hand-in-hand through the daisies. How idyllic it sounds. But that kind of relationship rarely lasts, although it went on for quite a time, right into our twenties in fact. We were besotted with each other.'

Shelley smiled gently. Her godmother was given to extravagant discourse and there was no getting away from the fact that she was a trifle eccentric.

Lorraine looked up. 'Your mother was a lovely woman. You take after her. The moment Frank met her he was lost.'

Shelley detected the trace of irony that still remained after all this time. Her mother and godmother had been close friends, working for the same model agency. It had been Lorraine who had introduced Angela to Frank.

A year later Lorraine had been assigned to model diamond necklaces at the Amsterdam trade fair and that was where she had met Karel.

Lorraine looked away suddenly. 'Karel used to tease me about my childhood sweetheart, but he never stopped me from seeing Frank and Angela and the four of us remained...friends.'

'I'm glad,' said Shelley, noting the slight hesitation.

'It was tragic for Angela to die in that influenza epidemic. Then for me to lose Karel in the yacht accident...' Lorraine rose and went towards the door. 'And now they're going to dig it all up again.'

Shelley let the Commandant's golden retriever off the lead and stood in her favourite spot at the edge of the dunes. As she watched, the blood-red sun slid into the darkening sea, turning it to molten gold and leaving tangled streaks of orange and pink, like gossamer threads trailing across the sky. The sun looked so hot she almost expected it to hiss as it touched the water.

Breathing in the perfume of the pines that marked the boundary of the hotel grounds she felt marvellous. She had laid the ghost of her lost lover and this precious freedom seemed a tangible quality.

Presently the new moon rose, a thin silver crescent lying on its back—like a heavenly smile, she thought! And she remembered her grandmother's warning, when the new moon rises on its back watch out for stormy days ahead.

She was startled by a low growl from the dog and turned apprehensively to see a shadow move beside a bush.

'Bello! Come here!' she called, relieved when the dog obediently returned to her side.

'Good boy!' She clipped the lead on as the tall figure of Dirk Joustra stepped into the moonlight.

'Good evening, Miss Pearson.'

She wondered if he had seen her leave the hotel to take the dog for its customary walk, and followed her.

He stared out over the sea. 'Bad moon rising. Rough weather ahead when the moon grins.'

She was surprised he knew the old wives' tale. 'What are you doing here?' she asked vexedly.

'It's a free country.'

'Not for me apparently.' She was jerked forward as the dog strained towards Dirk. 'I can't talk with whom I please. I can't take the dog out without being followed. Did you think I was sneaking out to meet Ryder?'

'No, he's in the bar.'

'I suppose you've come to warn me off him again,' she said acidly. 'Well, it may surprise you to know I want nothing more to do with him. As you said, it's over.'

He took the lead from her hand and matched his steps to hers as she headed back to the hotel.

'What happened?' he asked huskily. 'Want to tell me?'

His sympathetic tone threw her off guard. 'Nothing to tell.' She trailed her hand in the tall spiky grasses growing beside the path. Then, 'We were engaged. Ryder broke it off because he didn't...love me any more.'

'Did the collapse of your father's firm have anything to do with Ryder's change of heart?'

'Maybe.'

He frowned. 'I don't like what you're saying. My sister is a delicate creature. She was crippled from a gymnasium accident in her early teens. If Ryder's as shallow as you're implying then he's not at all the kind of husband I would have chosen for her.'

Shelley gathered her wits. Ryder wasn't her problem any more. And Dirk's description of his sister made her heart overflow with pity. Tilda sounded vulnerable. The last thing she wanted was to spoil the marriage—and an interfering brother wasn't going to help Tilda.

'Listen, Dirk. Ryder and I had something once then it died. It doesn't mean he doesn't love your sister.'

'I hope you're right.' Dirk looked sideways at her in the dusky twilight. 'Are you sure you're over him? When you met him again you looked as though you'd been struck by lightning. And last night you weren't exactly pushing him away.'

'He was just being friendly.'

'I know what I saw.'

'Have it your way.'

In silence, they crossed the lawn to a wrought-iron gate leading to the courtyard.

As Shelley lifted the latch, Dirk placed his hand under her elbow. 'Keep away from him, Shelley. Tilda needs him. If you want a bit of fun, have it with me.'

She thought she hadn't heard him properly and stood there staring open-mouthed. Then she burst out laughing at the absurdity of his suggestion. 'Not my idea of fun!'

'How do you know? You haven't tried me.' He went on earnestly. 'Or perhaps you just want to get your own back, to even the score with Ryder. Well, there again, I'm your man.'

She saw the flash of his teeth in the light from the overhanging coach-lamp. 'Heavens! The male ego sure takes some beating. Just when I think it's imaginary after all, it comes galloping up again, firing on all cylinders.'

'You do mix your metaphors.' He looped the lead over one of the spikes on the gate and sliced his fingers into her long hair. 'But the lady protests too much.'

She could see clearly the network of little lines beside his eyes, the smudgy effect of his thick dark-gold lashes, the scar on his angular cheek. His glance played over her like a searchlight, setting her nerves prickling and a convulsive shiver sliding down her spine.

He eased her into his arms and brought his mouth to hers. At first his kiss was playful, then his lips grew more persistent till she felt heat radiating through her limbs and saw lights bursting beneath her closed eyelids.

The power this stranger had over her made no sense but she was forced to concede she had been waiting for this contact with him from the instant they had met. It was as if her emotions had been simmering on a low gas and were suddenly turned up to full heat.

'There.' The word reverberated against her trapped mouth before he drew away from her.

They gazed at each other.

Shelley was vaguely aware of the dog whimpering, a church bell ringing, the birds twittering in the trees, but could not drag her eyes away from the fount of her bewilderment. It was like being under the influence of a sorcerer. Later she was to ponder the empathy which flowed between them, linking them together in that timeless moment.

He blinked and the spell was broken. 'That's just for starters, to keep you wanting more.'

She brought her unharnessed thoughts in line. Her new-found independence was a joy to her, something she had earned through suffering and disillusionment. She wasn't going to throw it all away now. 'Well, really!'

'I'll help you forget Ryder.'

'I've already forgotten.' Forgiven yes, but it would take time to forget what she had been through. 'Don't do me any favours. Please.'

His slow smile dawned. *'Goede nacht, Mejuffrouw.'*

He was swallowed up by the night and she felt like a traveller in an alien land, off the beaten track, without a road map...

'Oh Bello.' She fondled the animal's silky ears. 'He'll need watching.' Shakily she added, 'So will I!'

CHAPTER 4

Granny's weather lore was on target. A couple of days later a gale lashed the western shores of Holland and one of the beech trees was blown across the back door of the bungalow. Shelley and Lorraine spent the morning lopping the branches and clearing up the damage.

Lorraine was preoccupied as they worked. The salvage team had commenced diving and found nothing and the gale should postpone any further operations for a while.

Shelley had been wary of meeting Dirk

again after that kiss in the moonlight and was glad when she discovered he was working. But now he would be hanging round the hotel again and she was bound to bump into him. When she arrived for duty she saw him and Greet sharing a pot of coffee in the lounge, flaxen head and ginger close together as they talked and laughed.

She crept away to where Ryder was propping up the bar, a pensive look on his face, a gin and tonic in his hand.

He frowned at her. 'I waited in the Noordzee bar the other night but you didn't come. How about a stroll along the beach?'

'Can't you see I'm working?'

He trailed her into the corridor. 'We used to enjoy walking along windy beaches. Remember?'

She remembered all right and a lump caught in her throat. She swallowed it determinedly. 'Things are different now. My life has changed. And you're married.'

He watched her sort the towels in the laundry cupboard. 'I was going to tell you. I was waiting for the right moment. My wife...'

'Is Dirk's sister. He told me.'

'I know what you're thinking.'

'Do you? How clever of you!'

'It isn't like that. I care for her very much.'

'Then why are you pursuing me?' She took an armful of fluffy towels in her arms.

'Pursuing you? A walk along the beach for old time's sake? I'd like a chance to explain things, that's all.'

'I don't want to hear any of your explanations.' She pushed past him. 'And whatever would Dirk say?'

'He doesn't own me.' Ryder bounded after her. 'Besides he needn't know.'

As she stepped into the lift she experienced a twinge of disgust and her thoughts were registered on her face.

'Don't get me wrong!' he said. 'You do have a poor opinion of me.'

'With good reason.'

'I love my wife,' he insisted. 'She's so different from you...' He looked embarrassed. 'Sorry, that wasn't meant to sound rude.'

'Yes, she's got connections,' Shelley couldn't resist saying, 'I haven't.'

'You're so wrong. I knew for a long time it wouldn't work for us, long before Frank lost the firm. I tried to tell you several times but you wouldn't listen. In the end I had to be brutally honest.'

'You make me sound like a first-class idiot.'

'You were young. I was sorry for you.'

A fresh wave of misery caught her amidships. 'Great!' She pressed the button and the lift doors closed smartly, before Ryder could gain admittance. When she stepped out on the top floor she saw him leaping up the last few stairs.

'You can't escape me. I intend to say my piece. I've thought about you often, but knew I'd hurt you and was nervous of contacting you again.'

'You nervous, Ryder? I can't believe it.'

She made directly for the sauna but he nipped in front of her and stretched his arm across the door.

'You've grown cynical, my dear. It doesn't suit you. Let's leave the cynicism to Dirk Joustra.' His eyes narrowed. 'Or have you fallen for him?'

The heat rose to her cheeks. 'Don't be ridiculous!'

'If you're looking for romance there you'll be disappointed,' grunted Ryder. 'He's a cold fish, like most Dutchmen.

They marry late, after sowing their wild oats, then settle for a marriage contract with as much sensitivity as a farmer buying a good brood mare. There's an ancient rhyme which sums them up pretty well.
"In matters of commerce, the fault of the Dutch
Is offering too little and asking too much."
It applies to affairs of the heart too, I believe.'

'Thanks for the warning.'

'Friesians marry Friesians.'

'Tilda didn't.'

'There was strong family opposition, I can tell you.' His mouth twisted sarcastically. 'Dirk will take one of his own kind for a wife. A nice, placid, well-balanced girl. Not someone like you, Shelley. You're too hung-up.'

'And whose fault is that?'

'Not mine! You were too possessive. Oh, I understood. You lost your mother at a critical age after being the adored only child. But you fouled me up real good.'

'I fouled you up!'

'Yeah!' He grinned suddenly. 'So watch your step, my dear. I only have your welfare at heart...'

She ducked under his arm and entered

the steamy little anteroom where several people sat about, robed in towels.

Ryder raised his arms helplessly and ambled away.

She was shaking inwardly from his verbal onslaught. It had taken six months to erase her memories of him but seeing him again had brought them all flooding back. She was more resolved than ever to be vigilant where men were concerned.

'I shall offer Mr Joustra money to call off the search,' said Lorraine suddenly over dinner.

'A bribe?' gasped Shelley. 'You're not serious.'

'Not a bribe,' Lorraine insisted, 'Compensation for his trouble, repayment for his expenses.' She ticked them off on her fingers. 'Bringing the salvage vessel here, hiring the van, the cost of the hotel rooms...'

Greet snorted. 'And where will you get the money? Considering how badly Papa was insured. Surely you don't intend using...' She broke off and darted a guarded look in Shelley's direction.

Lorraine cut in hastily, 'I shall sell the bungalow.'

Greet laughed scornfully. 'The diamonds are worth a million pounds. He's not likely to give up the search for the comparatively small sum the bungalow will fetch.'

'The diamonds are a bird in the bush,' said Lorraine. 'He may never find them. Cash would be a bird in the hand. There are plenty of other wrecks for him to salvage.'

'And where will you live?' enquired Greet. 'I've given up the house in Nice so you can't come there.'

Lorraine said airily, 'I haven't worked out the details yet, but I'll think of something. That yacht is your father's grave. It must be respected.' Another veiled look passed between them and Shelley was puzzled.

'But Papa wouldn't want you to respect it to the extent of losing your home,' reasoned Greet. 'Be realistic!'

'My mind's made up,' said Lorraine. 'Shelley, my dear, you must put the proposition to Mr Joustra in the morning.'

'Me?' Shelley choked on a mouthful of wine. 'Why me?'

'The man's obviously attracted, my dear. The offer would look best coming from you.'

'No really, I couldn't. In any case, he won't accept. He'll just make me feel stupid.'

'You will do it.' Lorraine covered Shelley's hand with her own. 'For me. Because of our friendship.'

Shelley shook her head wordlessly.

'And because you have some connection with all this, indirectly, remembering it was Frank's yacht which...'

Shelley felt awful. How could she refuse now? It was blackmail, but she couldn't condemn Lorraine for resorting to it. The woman looked so frail and defeated these days. All the same she wasn't looking forward to going to Dirk with such a preposterous offer.

He was sitting on a bench in the courtyard out of the wind which was still strong enough to prevent any diving.

He didn't notice her approaching and she feasted her eyes on him, observing the way the breeze tugged at his hair and the determined slant of his mouth. That mouth, which had wreaked such havoc to her senses when it had governed her own so totally!

Her shadow fell across him and he looked up.

She came straight to the point. 'Mrs van Hoorn really doesn't want her husband's grave disturbed. She's willing to compensate you if you'll agree to give up the search.'

He rose to his feet. 'And what price has she in mind?'

'I don't know. She talked about selling the bungalow.'

'Sounds drastic. I wonder why she feels compelled to go to such lengths.'

'She told you! Karel's grave is important to her.'

'Really. She sounds like a devoted widow.'

Shelley ignored his tone of derision. 'Look, you've no guarantee of success. Why not cut your losses and take the money?'

Her squinted at her. 'Is that your advice?'

'No!' The word was out before she could prevent it. 'I mean, I don't think she should sell her home, but I understand her feelings. She loved Karel and was shattered by his death. Why, she's made a shrine out of his study.' She bit her lip, wishing she hadn't divulged such a personal detail of Lorraine's grief.

'Has she now!' He shook his head. 'I'm

sorry, but that's not the way I work. I'm into salvage not bribery.'

'Compensation,' corrected Shelley.

'Call it what you will, it's out of the question. I can't have grieving widows selling their homes on my account. I hope I have more integrity than that.'

'Integrity! In your line of business?' She laughed harshly. 'Robbing graves?'

'Come now. You're being melodramatic.'

'Robbing graves,' she repeated. 'Picking over old wrecks like a glorified rag and bone man. Like a vulture.' She knew she was going over the top but had failed Lorraine and wanted to take her inadequacy out on him. 'Like a jackal!'

He said levelly, 'It has to be done. Some cargoes are positively dangerous. The environment can't be left littered or the world would soon grind to a halt. Vultures and jackals are the most important creatures in the jungle. They clear up the mess. On consideration I have no objection to being likened to them.'

She felt chastened and turned away dejectedly.

'Cheer up!' He gave his familiar chuckle. 'You did your best.' His hand smoothed the back of her hair. 'You're a loyal little godchild.'

She jerked her head away. 'I'm very attached to Lorraine. She's been wonderful to me, giving me a home, helping me put my life into perspective.'

'Okay, okay. You don't have to justify your motives to me. Loyalty is a quality I admire. It's just a pity yours is so misplaced.'

'Oh, what's the use! You don't know what you're talking about.'

'On the contrary, I think I do.'

He watched her for an interminable time and she felt the dynamic pull of his cornflower eyes, bewitching her again.

'You're probably loyal to your father too, but you have a sneaking suspicion he might have been responsible for Karel's death. Am I right?'

She quaked at his perception. How was it a stranger could see so clearly what she barely saw herself?

He went on imperturbably, 'I've never met your father, but I've heard of him. He's a fine engineer...'

'Don't patronise me, Mr Joustra!'

'He invented a buoyancy tank that was going to revolutionise sailing—a dream many engineers have nursed. New tanks come out every year. They're ten a penny...'

'He's a crank, you mean?'

'Let me finish!' He ran impatient fingers through his fringe. 'Who's to say he failed? The fact is his theory was never tested.'

'Not tested?' She raised her voice. 'You call a sunken yacht and a dead man not tested?'

'Until we find out how the yacht sank we must give him the benefit of the doubt.'

'That's not what his creditors and backers thought!'

'Didn't you have any faith in his invention?'

Oh, that was beneath the belt! 'Of course I did!'

'Then why don't you want me to find the yacht?'

She opened her mouth—and shut it again. All he said was true. But she was torn between Lorraine's feelings and her father's reputation. Suddenly she wanted the yacht found—even if it proved her father's invention was worthless. Anything would be better than this uncertainty. But she couldn't go behind Lorraine's back and say so.

His expression softened and she had an idea he understood anyway.

'Salvage men aren't grave despoilers. We won't disturb the remains. We'll take the diamonds, examine the yacht and leave everything as we find it. I promise.'

There was nothing more to be said. Shelley began to walk away but Dirk called out to her.

'Hang on, Shelley. I've ordered a car from the hotel with you as driver.'

Her jaw dropped. 'Sorry?'

'You heard me.'

'What do you need a car for? Where's the hired van?'

'Henk has it.'

She knew that was a lie, she'd seen Henk and Ryder go off on foot along the beach, fishing rods in their hands. She racked her brains for an excuse, 'You can drive. Why do you need me? I don't feel like driving today.'

'It's no good. I've booked a chauffeur-driven car and you're the driver. Why don't you check?'

She knew that would be a pointless operation and glared at him. 'All right. Where are we going?'

'I'll tell you later.' He sounded apologetic

now he'd got his way. 'I know you find my company irksome, but it won't take long.'

'I didn't say that.'

'No, but you've made it patently clear where I stand in your popularity poll. Marginally below Dracula and the monster from outer space, I'd say.'

She didn't contradict him. 'I'll get my blazer.'

'No!' He actually looked embarrassed. 'Change into something nice.'

'What are you up to?'

'Oh, do as you're told!'

She gave a sloppy salute. 'Yes sir!'

Lorraine was in Shelley's room, dusting. 'Did you see Joustra? What did he say?'

'He wouldn't make a deal.' Shelley's voice was muffled as she pulled a woollen dress, patterned in large squares of saffron and lilac, over her head. 'He implied it would ruin his reputation.'

'Huh!' Lorraine zipped up the dress for her. 'What reputation? He's a crook. He let his partner go to prison for a crime he committed himself...'

'Calm down, dear.' Shelley rummaged in the wardrobe for a chunky metal belt and a pair of high heels. 'You don't know that. I'm sure you're worrying needlessly.' She grabbed a champagne-coloured coat and matching bag and rushed outside.

Five minutes later she drove the Citroën out of the hotel garage. Dirk climbed in beside her but they hadn't gone half a mile before he ordered her to stop and took over the controls himself.

'Why did you want a driver if you intended driving yourself?' she complained, groping for the seat belt.

'I didn't.' He turned the car south-east. 'But you'll never drive in those heels!'

'Where are we going, for Pete's sake?'

'I'm taking you out for the day.' He put his foot down hard. 'There's nothing you can do about it.'

She grinned suddenly. 'You are the limit.'

'Aren't I? We're going to see the bulbfields. You said you'd never been.'

'Well, I've been working hard,' she defended herself. 'And when I used to visit the van Hoorns it was always summer, not the best time to see the blooms.'

'I wouldn't say that. There's always something to see in the fields of Holland.' He shot her an enquiring glance. 'You must know the van Hoorns well. What was Karel like?'

'A pretty average Dutchman!'

'No such animal!' He smirked. 'Seriously though.'

'Quiet and studious, I suppose. And secretive. I didn't know him all that well. He was sort of background.'

'Could he have perpetrated a fraud?'

'No!'

'Because he was a family friend?'

She shrugged. 'You won't believe me whatever I say.'

'Haven't you wondered at the various motives he might have had?'

'Of course,' she replied wearily. 'Speculation was rife at the time. But nothing added up. I mean, if he'd planned to disappear, why didn't he take out a hefty insurance policy?'

'Perhaps he was too clever for that.'

'I don't understand.'

'No, you're too nice.'

They approached Alsmeer, driving between acres of hothouses and nurseries. Dirk parked the car and took her to see one of the famous auction warehouses, the whole place haunted by the scent of thousands of irises for sale.

The auctioneer set in motion what looked like a vast clock with numbers round the rim representing prices for the batches of flowers similar to a sample being displayed. The numbers in the centre of the dial corresponded to the seats where the buyers sat, Dirk explained.

The building buzzed with excited conversation as a pointer, like a huge minute-hand, began to move, beginning at high prices and working backwards. The instant it reached a price acceptable to the most eager buyer, he pressed his electric button, the pointer stopped and the number of his seat lit up on the clock-face. The batch was his.

'At last I know the meaning of a Dutch auction,' said Shelley.

They stayed half an hour while six hundred lots were sold and she was impressed by the fairness and efficiency of the system.

'That's nothing,' said Dirk. 'Ten of those clocks are continuously in operation.'

They drove westward towards Sassenheim, travelling alongside chequer-board fields of daffodils, tulips and hyacinths, a man-made tide of colour reaching as far as the eye could see.

They came to a floral mosaic in the shape of a windmill which had been worked out petal by petal and mounted on a huge board. Dirk pulled up beside a group of children who were making the discarded blooms into garlands to sell to passers-by.

He called out in Dutch, 'I wonder which of you can find me a bunch of hyacinths to match this lady's fascinating eyes.' He added, 'There's twenty florins in it.'

Shelley blushed as half a dozen children pushed their heads into the car to stare at her, then proceeded to hold up various blooms, arguing vociferously.

The final contest was between two bunches of deep blue. Dirk deliberated before choosing the deepest and handing over the reward to a young girl who squealed with delight.

Shelley accepted the bell-shaped flowers and inhaled their heady perfume. 'They're lovely! Thank you!'

There was a warm glow in his eyes and she felt a shiver uncurl down her spine as she foundered in the slipstream of his magnetic personality again.

'It's twelve-thirty.' He nodded towards

a roadside restaurant. 'Shall we take *koffietafel?*'

'Dutch treat?'

'Certainly not!'

The restaurant, called *Klompenhuis*, was hung with hundreds of wooden shoes, all colours and sizes.

As they took their seats in a sunny window overlooking a field of goats, Shelley mused, 'How is it the businesslike Dutch always make it look as if they are only concerned with rural pursuits?'

It was a rhetorical question, but Dirk answered her. 'We've never lost track of our bucolic roots and are proud of our heritage. Because we've waged war with nature for the land, it's of prime importance to us.'

Lunch in Holland was a light informal meal consisting of various kinds of open sandwiches. They ordered *uitsmijter*—fried eggs on slices of cold beef on buttered bread, with centre dishes of salad and tiny smoked sausages.

In accordance with Dutch tradition, Dirk helped Shelley to the food, picking out the choicest bits for her. She liked this custom and presently did the same for him.

Taking up his fork, he glanced at a

dense cluster of wooden shoes above their heads. 'I hope they're securely anchored. My sister and I used to throw *klompens* at each other and I've still got the scars to prove it.'

'Any brothers and sisters apart from Tilda?' she asked as the coffee arrived.

Mouth full, he shook his head.

'You must be close,' she said with the wistfulness of an only child, 'I envy you.'

'Yes, we are.'

'You said Tilda was crippled in a gym accident. How did it happen?'

Dirk picked up his glass and looked out of the window, giving the distinct impression he did not wish to discuss the matter. Then he said, 'She was training for the human pyramid when she...fell. She's seen several leading physicians but she remains lame.'

Shelley nodded sympathetically.

'It turned her from a sunny girl to a brooding introvert. One doctor even suggested it was psychosomatic. I confess I was worried when she met and married Ryder, but the change in her has been wonderful to see.'

'I'm glad.'

'She was a first-class diver and I had

intended making her a partner in the firm. But the accident changed all that. So I made Ryder a partner instead. Not only is he experienced under water, he's good with the paperwork. His devious mind is quite unnerving.'

'Yes.' Shelley didn't want to talk about Ryder. 'And what about the rest of your family? Your parents?'

'My mother lives with me in Friesland. My father died many years ago. He was also an expert diver.'

'Do you dive yourself?'

'Of course.' He smiled slyly. 'Expertly.'

'But you're the boss. You don't have to dive.'

'I enjoy it. I don't get much chance these days. I travel a lot making the arrangements. This current search is comparatively simple and I was determined to take part. After all we don't want to bring up the yacht, just the diamonds.'

'It sounds interesting. And dangerous.'

'Not if you know what you're doing. Our last job was salvaging historical remains from a treasure ship which sank in the Med in 1853. So you see, we don't just rob graves.'

She could see her earlier taunts still

rankled and she relented. 'All right, I admit the necessity for salvage.'

The waitress hovered and they ordered a pancake. It arrived, a foot across, filled with apple syrup and smothered with cream.

'Hm, I'll have to watch my figure,' she murmured.

'Looks perfect to me.' His eyelids drooped lazily and his eyes seemed to reach out and touch her body, lingering on the small firm swell of her breasts outlined under the saffron and lilac squares. 'You're so petite and well-proportioned, you make me feel like King Kong.'

'Just as long as there's no monkey business,' she parried.

He ordered a glass of curacao for her and she sipped it slowly, savouring the taste of oranges. 'Aren't you having one?'

'No, I'm driving.' He poured himself another coffee. 'Now, tell me about you. All I know is you're Frank Pearson's daughter.'

'Oh, my life is pretty ordinary,' she demurred. 'I grew up in Tilbury, the very happy, very spoiled only child. My days were filled with ballet lessons and riding and Girl Guides. All the usual things. My mother was a model but she gave it up when I was born. She passed on all her modelling tips to me, how to walk gracefully, how to use make-up, how to buy clothes wisely.' Shelley's eyes clouded. 'She died of influenza when I was fourteen.'

'I'm sorry.'

'It was a shattering experience, to lose someone without warning like that. One day she was there, the next gone. I took it badly. She was my world. For ages I couldn't bear to let Daddy out of my sight in case he was snatched away too.'

He patted her hand as it lay on the table. 'Do you take after her?'

'Daddy says so.'

'She must have been beautiful.'

Their gaze met and held. As she stared into the depths of his eyes she felt she was drowning and grew giddy from the sensual undercurrents eddying about her.

They both jumped as the waitress presented the bill.

Shelley hastily withdrew her hand and glanced away, her limbs trembling. Did he look at all women like that? If so, they didn't stand a chance. Correction. *She* didn't stand a chance.

She went to the ladies' room to freshen

up and when she returned Dirk was holding her coat. As she eased her arms into the sleeves he said, 'Come along now, we've still got a lot to see.'

'Oh?' His hands glanced the back of her neck and a curious ache throbbed through her. 'I...think I'd better be getting back to the hotel.'

'Don't worry. I told the Commandant I needed the car all day.'

She glanced at him sharply. He was jutting his chin in an imperious manner and his cornflower eyes defied any argument. 'You've got a nerve!'

He relaxed his taut expression and grinned. 'Yes, I think you can safely say that.'

CHAPTER 5

The road led them to Lisse in the heart of the bulbfields where daffodils and irises marched across the low fen in serried ranks of yellow and blue. As the wind rippled their heads like wavelets on a great lake, it seemed the dykes had burst their banks with a flood of flowers instead of water.

'You're in for a treat,' said Dirk, pulling in to the car park outside the *Keukenhof Gardens*.

'Kitchen gardens?' she asked. 'It seems a strange name for a floral exhibition.'

'Ah, Jacoba of Bavaria, the tragic fifteenth-century countess, who's a favourite with all Dutch schoolkids, used to ride here with her falconers. These were the kitchen gardens of her hunting lodge.'

They joined a group waiting to be shown round by one of the *meisjes*—young women guides dressed in the traditional hunting costume of green jacket, bustled skirt and tall riding hat.

The tour began in front of Countess Jacoba's statue.

'She was the only daughter of William the Sixth, Duke of Bavaria and Count of Holland,' the *meisje* recited. 'She reigned in 1418 but met opposition from the nobles who refused to recognise a woman as their liege.' She spread her arms expressively. 'Men can be so difficult.'

Everybody laughed.

'They plotted to betray her and she was left powerless. The poor girl was only seventeen and already a widow. She

90

had two more tragic marriages—first to the Dauphine of France then to the English Duke of Gloucester, before she found happiness with Count Van Borssele. She died at thirty-two. What you might call a short but eventful life.'

Shelley was intrigued to discover an English connection and asked Dirk which Duke of Gloucester was involved.

'Don't ask me. What do I know about English history? Didn't you learn about him at school?'

'I didn't learn about all the dukes,' she protested. 'There were hundreds of them. Most of them obscure. What year would that have been?'

'1422?'

'That could have been Humphrey Plantagenet.'

'Oh, I've heard of him,' said Dirk blithely. 'Good Duke Humphrey!'

Shelley grimaced. 'I wouldn't say that. If Jacoba was in fact his duchess, he had the marriage annulled after six years, then married his mistress, Eleanor something —or—other, who was reputed to be a witch.'

'Takes all sorts,' muttered Dirk.

They strolled between flower beds skirting

a picturesque lake. Eight million bulbs blossomed in the sixty-acre estate, but it was impossible to see all but a small part of it in one afternoon.

In one of the hothouses were the famous snow-white amaryllis and pink calla lilies which had been originally produced there and the air was cloying with the trapped scents.

The tour ended at the Queen Juliana Pavilion, a glass-fronted building crammed with shrubs and pot plants, where Shelley bought a china *klompen* filled with budding pinks for Lorraine.

As they got back in the car she felt pleasantly tired and dozed all the way to the hotel.

'Come on, sleepy-head.'

She opened her eyes to see Dirk gazing down at her intently. Before she could take evasive action, his hands cupped her cheeks and his mouth swooped towards her. 'Shelley, you are beautiful.'

She wriggled uncomfortably, 'Don't...'

'Aw come on. One little kiss..'

'So it's to be Dutch treat after all?'

'For Pete's sake!' He pulled her roughly into his arms and lowered his lips to begin a heart-stopping tour over her brow, down the side of her face and into the hollows of her neck. Finally his mouth moved over hers, dragging against her lips, feathering but never quite kissing her, promising but withholding the fulfilment of that promise, till she ached with longing.

She was submerged once more in the sexual aura of him—the sound of his breathing, the tang of his mouth and the smooth texture of his leather jacket.

When she thought she was to remain in this kind of limbo for ever, his mouth crushed hers, sending her brain reeling and splinters of excitement crackling through her bloodstream. She returned his kiss with abandonment, felt the flames of desire, faint at first then growing stronger, licking through her nervous system like a slow burning fuse.

'Shelley,' he breathed. 'Am I reading you right?'

His words jolted her back to sanity and she was frightened of the emotions he had unleashed in her. Oh yes, it would be easy to lose herself in this man's arms, but a short-lived fling with a stranger wasn't what she wanted. She had the sense to know only heartache lay along that route, because he was the kind of man she could fall in love with, sooner or later. If she didn't want her heart trampled again—and God knew she didn't—then she had to call a halt to this madness now, while she still had time, before she had reached the point of no return.

She pulled back from him. 'That's enough!'

'What's up? Can't trust yourself?'

'Something like that.'

He shook his head. 'I could have sworn you were giving me the green light. I wish you wouldn't mess me about like this. I don't know whether I'm coming or going.'

Welcome to the club, she thought, opening the door.

Standing on the forecourt, he studied her as the breeze stirred and toyed with her hair. 'There's a fire in you. You can't deny it. But you sure know how to put a man down.'

'I'm sorry. It's not your fault. It's just that I'm not ready for...all that...'

'Is that a fact?' He sounded annoyed and she couldn't blame him.

He studied the sky. 'The wind's dropped. We might be able to continue the search tomorrow. Will you have dinner with me afterwards?'

'I don't think that would be a good idea.' She remembered her manners. 'Thanks...for the lunch...and the flowers...'

'My pleasure!'

Greet, looking peeved, was in the bungalow garden. 'You've been out with Dirk. The Commandant told me he'd hired you for the day.'

'Would you like to rephrase that?'

'I only want to know where I stand. Either I'm welcome to him or I'm not.'

Shelley bit her lower lip.

'I notice you're not coming back with your usual reply.' Greet shrugged her elegant shoulders. 'Why don't we go into Zandvoort this evening and paint the town red?'

'I'm tired.'

'We used to have good times together. We're not going to fall out over Dirk Joustra, are we?'

'Of course not, but I really am tired. Another time.'

The weather settled and Shelley saw little of Dirk for the next couple of weeks. At first he invited her for a drink after each day's diving but after she declined three times he stopped asking. It hadn't escaped her notice that he spent most evenings with Greet in the hotel lounge and once she saw them dancing together in the ballroom.

Mid May brought a most welcome letter from Shelley's father. He sounded in good spirits and although the work was gruelling he was setting aside a tidy sum in the bank. He enclosed a gold necklace he had picked up in a bazaar and expressed interest in her news that a salvage firm was investigating the sinking of the yacht.

One fine morning Shelley was checking a delivery of beer in the courtyard when Dirk came out to stow some equipment into the hired van.

He shouted a greeting.

She signed the lorry driver's docket and the man climbed into his cab. As the vehicle pulled away she walked over to Dirk. 'How's the search going? Making any progress?'

'We've drawn a blank so far, but who knows? Today could be the day.' His gaze roved over her sawn-off jeans and jungle-print shirt, the ends of which she had knotted in front, exposing her midriff. She'd been working in the cellar where her uniform was impracticable.

'Why the sudden concern?' he asked.

She fingered the thin strand of gold at her throat, 'I've heard from Daddy and he's interested in the outcome.'

Dirk stroked his chin thoughtfully. 'How would you like to come out in the salvage vessel and witness the operation for yourself? Then you can write to Frank and put him in the picture.'

She viewed him circumspectly. 'You're joking!'

'No, I mean it. Come and spend the day with us. You'll find it fascinating, I guarantee. After all, you have a vested interest.'

She considered the prospect. It would be nice. And she was off work in ten minutes. But...being with Dirk all day? That was something else. Remembering his kisses and her reaction to them. However they wouldn't be alone. Ryder and Henk would be there. She banished her reservations. 'Okay.'

Dirk grinned. 'Right! Be ready in five minutes.' Another glance at her apparel. 'Come as you are.'

By the time she had dashed across to the bungalow for her jacket and bag, Ryder and Henk had put in an appearance.

The latter was plainly surprised to learn

she was joining them and he darted speculative glances from her to Dirk and back again.

'You do cooking, yes okay please, Miss Pearson?' asked Henk hopefully in his fractured English. 'Make morning drinks and lunch also, what say you?'

She nodded. 'I'd love to. I want to do my share.'

'Good,' said Ryder. 'The meals are Henk's department and he's not exactly *cordon bleu,* whereas I recall you throw a tasty dish together.' He winked then saw Dirk's disapproving gaze and cleared his throat noisily. 'All the ingredients are there.' He indicated a basket of food in the back of the van. 'Nothing fancy, we usually have soup and open sandwiches with plenty of protein to keep us fit and warm under water.'

Shelley checked the contents. 'I can do better than that. Why don't we stop at the market so I can get some things.'

It was agreed and they piled into the van.

They eventually reached the shore where a small inflated dinghy with an outboard motor was beached. Henk took the controls and, with spindrift breaking over them like

98

rain, they skimmed over the sparkling water to the salvage vessel moored a hundred yards offshore.

Shelley nimbly climbed the ladder hanging over the side but was glad of Dirk's hand to haul her over the gunwale.

The vessel was smaller than she had envisaged, a twenty foot motor launch with a cabin and tiny galley, and the deck contained a wealth of equipment, such as oxygen cylinders, a compressor for filling air bottles and an echo sounder situated amidships. With Henk again at the wheel they set off for deeper waters and presently reached the yellow buoy marking the search area, some six miles from land.

A few battered canvas chairs stood on the deck and, as there was no hurry to start the cooking, Shelley made herself comfortable, prepared to watch the proceedings.

The glare from the sea was dazzling and the sun was hot. Summer had slipped in by the back door, she thought, donning her sunglasses.

Ryder handed her a yachting cap which she set at a jaunty angle on the back of her head. She had no need for lotions, her creamy skin took kindly to the sun and was already tanning nicely.

Dirk and Henk went below to change and emerged wearing orange and black wetsuits with cylinders strapped to their backs. They sat on the gunwale listening to the bleeps of the proton magnetometer and watching the wavy lines snaking across the screen, while Ryder steered the boat on a zigzag course over the water which was fifty-feet deep here.

Shelley had been brought up with boats and knew the drill. They would sail slowly, dragging the boom-rigged sonar 'fish' just above the ocean floor so that sound waves struck and penetrated the bottom, returning a description to the deck recorder in the form of graphs. These graphs could be interpreted by skilled readers, providing slight changes in wind and current were taken into account.

A second device, a side-scan, was also used to 'see' abnormalities at a considerable distance on either side of its own path over the sea bed.

Whenever they recorded something un-usual Ryder anchored the boat while the other two went over the side together to investigate. The safety rule was always to leave one man on board and they had hoisted a blue and white flag which Shelley recognised as the 'I have a diver down' signal. It was a long laborious business and most of the time presented false trails—a shoal of fish or clumps of weed which had upset the rhythm of the sounder.

Their findings were entered on a sea chart and anything of special interest was written in a separate book in case it proved to be of value to the authorities. For instance, Shelley learned, the wing of a World War Two Spitfire had been found the previous day.

The first time Dirk prepared to go over the side backwards into the water, he ordered, 'Keep your mind on your work, Ryder.'

'He doesn't trust me one little bit since you appeared on the scene, Shelley,' said Ryder over his shoulder as he sat in front of the scanner, making notes. 'What have you been saying about me?'

'I've hardly discussed you and certainly said nothing derogatory,' she told him. 'But how about the plain unvarnished truth?'

'And what's that?' He swung round in his chair. 'Did you want me to marry you without loving you?'

'Why not? That was your plan all along.'

'Was it? You don't know me at all.'

'I thought I did. I believed everything you said.'

'Everything you thought I said. I never lied to you. I did love you at the beginning. But it was a short-lived emotion. Even then, I still liked you a lot.'

She remembered the pain. 'And that's how you treat someone you like.'

'Oh Shelley, you were too possessive.' He tipped the chair back on two legs and laced his fingers behind his head. 'It was understandable, the way you clung to me as if your life depended on it. Frank explained it all to me, told me how you clung to him after your mother died. You must have ruined his love life! I think he was quite relieved when you transferred your dependence to me.'

'Ruined his love life? He had no love life.'

'Exactly.'

'How can you say that?' she burst out plaintively.

'All right, I take that back. But he was worried about you. From the start he encouraged our friendship. I tried to make it work for his sake.'

'How noble of you!'

'You switched your trust to me and I handled it all wrong,' he admitted sadly. 'I thought I loved you and had proposed before I realised my mistake. But I didn't want to hurt you so I bluffed my way through. I'm sorry. I wanted to go on loving you, but I couldn't love to order.'

She was stung by his outspokenness and needed to hurt back. 'But you really love Tilda!'

'Yes.' His tone softened. 'I really love Tilda.'

'And the fact she is Dirk's sister has nothing to do with it.'

'Nothing.' There was a tender glow in his eyes. 'She isn't strong. I have an overwhelming desire to protect her.' He laughed dryly. 'I seem to attract that sort, first you, then Tilda...'

'Thanks!'

'... But I love Tilda. You'd better believe it.'

Shelley's nerves were raw. 'And what happened first, the romance or the job?'

'The job. When your father went under I was left out on a limb. I'd heard Joustra was expanding and decided to come over and offer my services.'

'So you ditched me and off you went.'

'I hated hurting you but time was of the essence. If I'd waited I'd have missed my opportunity to join Joustra.'

It sounded so callous and she gave a little choke.

'Well, I got the job,' he continued reflectively. 'I met Tilda later, at a meeting at Dirk's home in Friesland and must admit my first emotion was pity. She's lame, you see.'

'Yes, Dirk told me about the accident she had.'

'Is that all he told you?' Ryder's voice contained a trace of derision. 'Did he omit to say he was the one who dropped her?'

'Oh no...'

'Yep. Dirk was supposed to hand Tilda up to the top of the pyramid but he missed. Oh, there was a mix-up in the directions and it wasn't his fault. But he blames himself of course. And there goes one guilty fella.'

The silence was awesome, broken only by the drone of a lone plane high overhead and the gentle sigh of the wind.

As Shelley let Ryder's revelations sink in she was filled with compassion for Dirk. How he must have suffered, must still suffer, every time he saw his sister, knowing he was indirectly the cause of her affliction. How he must have wanted to stop the world and wind it back to that fateful day.

She knew what a powerful force guilt could be, knew all too well the pressures it brought. It sapped the strength from the soul and acted as a motivator for all kinds of doubts and justifications. She still shared her father's guilt for the sinking of the *Angela Rose* and the death of Karel van Hoorn.

She shivered and for an agonising moment prayed the yacht might never be found.

CHAPTER 6

'It's murky down there,' said Dirk when they broke off for coffee which Shelley had prepared in the poky galley.

As he lolled in the chair, she noted how the wetsuit moulded his lean figure to perfection. The dazzle of the sun-kissed water sent liquid highlights flitting across his gaunt cheeks and made his eyes appear very blue and vital, as if he were plugged into an electric generator.

She wondered what made him so attractive. He had two eyes, two lips, a nose, just like everyone else, he had the required number of limbs...

Taking a steadying breath she sat down, kicked off her sandals and curled her legs under her. The balmy weather reminded her of the happy times she had spent sailing with her parents. Angela had always been content to sit in the sun but Frank liked to be actively involved.

She frowned as she recalled Ryder's taunts about her clinging ways. She admitted she had been possessive towards her father but was sure she hadn't 'ruined his love life'. The thought of him wanting to bring a lady friend home had never entered her head. But she conceded he was comparatively young and, with his mane of dark hair and bushy moustache, rather good-looking.

She glanced across at Ryder, staring gloomily into his coffee mug. Now there was a handsome man! Was that all there was to him? A pretty face?

For the rest of the morning Henk stayed

on board while the others dived. He told Shelley about his fiancée, who lived in Limburg, and showed her several dog-eared photographs of a buxom fair-haired girl who looked about seventeen.

Shelley left him to go below to see about lunch, preparing the Dutch dishes as Lorraine had shown her. *Erwtensoep*—a thick pea soup served with smoked sausages and slices of brown bread, followed by *uitsmijter*—the traditional open sandwiches.

'That looks appetising,' said Dirk. 'And a vast improvement on the rubbish Henk churns out.'

'*Ja!*' agreed the burly young man good-humouredly.

After lunch it was Dirk's turn to remain on board.

'Another wasted day?' asked Shelley.

'Not at all.' He had stripped off the wetsuit to reveal a pair of swimming trunks. 'You need patience on this job, but no time is wasted. If, at the end of the day, we find nothing, we can say categorically the yacht is not in this particular area. That's progress.'

She didn't like to stare but discovered she could see him reflected in the stainless steel panel on the side of the scanner.

He looked magnificently virile, his body tanned and patterned with golden hair which became a tangled forest on his chest.

He chuckled. 'Everything to your taste, ma'am?'

'Sorry?' She jumped as his eyes met hers in the panel.

'You'll know me another time.'

She blushed furiously. 'I wasn't looking at you. You flatter yourself. Your conceit takes some getting used to.'

A subtle smile played about his lips and she felt her heart beat in rhythm with the soft thud of the wavelets against the side of the vessel.

Casting about desperately for something mundane to say she came up with, 'How did you get that scar on your cheek?'

'It wasn't a jealous lover, if that's what you're thinking.'

Apparently nothing was mundane. 'A harpoon gun?'

'Nothing so Moby Dickish. My partner, my *ex*-partner, tried to make off with a fortune in banknotes. I waylaid him and he pulled a knife on me.'

She recalled Lorraine's bitter tirade. 'My godmother said you were all in it together.

She implied you were the crook and your partner took the can back.'

'She would!'

Shelley went to lean on the rail and stare at the landmass of west Holland. 'So you're as pure as the driven snow?'

'In business dealings, yes.'

For some reason she wanted to believe him.

He stood behind her and slipped his hands round her bare midriff, his touch burning her skin. She was caught off guard and forgot this man was dangerous. As she leaned back against him she felt his soft breath tickling her earlobes. She looked over her shoulder into his face and saw his eyes were closed, his lashes lying like bronzed spikes on his tanned cheeks.

She swivelled round and his lips brushed hers. She was submerged once more in the heady mystique of him. He tasted salty and her nostrils were filled with the tang of the sea.

She wasn't prepared for his next move. As he began untying the knot holding the ends of her shirt together, a slim thread of alarm permeated her brain.

'Stop that!'

He arched his brows. 'Your mouth says

no but your body says yes.'

Colour tinged her cheeks and it was with immense relief she heard a splash and saw Ryder and Henk swing flippered feet over the gunwale. She was conscious of two pairs of inquisitive eyes on her as she retied the shirt.

Ryder removed his mask. 'Here, Shelley, I brought this up for you.' He tossed her a king whelk shell, beautifully sculptured with an elongated spire and deep orange interior.

She thanked him. After their parting she had looked back on his gifts with contempt, thinking of his calculated motives. But he had no reason to impress her now and she wondered if she had misjudged him.

'Find anything?' asked Dirk, adding sarcastically, 'Besides the shell, that is?'

'Not a thing.' Ryder shook his head sending a jet of water over the deck. 'Might as well call it a day.'

'No,' Dirk decided. 'I've a feeling Shelley will bring us luck. We'll carry on for another hour and Henk and I will be diving.'

'Suit yourself.' Ryder sat down to remove his flippers. 'But the light won't last much longer.'

Henk weighed the anchor and they cruised along again as Dirk keenly watched the screen of the echo sounder.

'Hold it!' he ordered after half an hour. 'There's something down there.' A few minutes later he and Henk disappeared over the side.

'Well, you don't waste any time, Shelley,' murmured Ryder. 'I hope you know what you're doing.'

'It's none of your business.'

'True.' He placed one bare foot on the deck's bottom rail. 'But I worry about you.'

'Why? I'm not your problem any more.'

'Force of habit.' He looked grim. 'What you don't need is another guy who is going to let you down.'

They remained there in silence till the light began to fade from the sky. Ryder, dressed in sweater and jeans, paced the deck, glancing at his watch from time to time, till his anxiety transmitted itself to Shelley.

She was just going to ask him if he thought everything was all right below when she heard a loud splashing and gurgling as Dirk and Henk bobbed up beside the boat.

They were both excited as they climbed aboard and Dirk couldn't get his mask off fast enough.

'There's a yacht down there, all right! It's standing on end, with its bow buried in the silt.'

'Identification?' Ryder enquired.

Dirk gestured towards a horse-shoe lifebelt which Henk had thrown on the deck. 'We ripped this from its rusted bracket. See for yourself.'

The lifebelt was badly warped with half of its lettering worn away. All that remained were the letters R-O-S-E T-I-L.

'The *Angela Rose* Tilbury, wouldn't you say?' asked Dirk.

'Wow-ee!' Ryder punched the air with his fist.

Shelley felt her scalp tingle and gave a little cry.

Dirk took her arm. 'Are you all right? Here, come and sit down. You've had a shock.' He pushed her gently into a chair. 'We can't do any more tonight. We'll leave the marker and come out first thing tomorrow.'

The sound of the radio cut across his words and Ryder leapt to pick up the headphones.

'Yes, this is the Joustra salvage vessel. Go ahead.' He picked up a pencil and began to scribble on a pad, a frown creasing his brow. A few moments later he switched off the transmitter, his face twisted with irony.

'Get a load of this! Mrs van Hoorn went to court this morning to enter a plea to have the diving stopped on compassionate grounds.'

'She what!' Dirk's eyes were ablaze with fury under their thick gold brows. 'Go on!'

Ryder glanced at the notepad. 'The court met at a special emergency sitting this afternoon. They agreed to look into the matter and give their verdict at a later date. Till then a diving ban is imposed. We are to return to Zandvoort immediately where an official of the court is waiting to deliver the necessary notice to us.'

Dirk hit his palm with his clenched fist. 'God! That woman! Is there no limit to what she'll do to have us abandon this search?' His eyes narrowed shrewdly. 'Well, it won't get her anywhere. We've found the yacht now and I shall go to court to fight her, first thing in the morning.'

This unexpected turn of events put a

damper on the team's spirits, and Dirk's expression as they drove to the hotel was dark and brooding.

'Now that the yacht has been located,' he said, 'Public opinion will be on our side. It's only human nature to want to know how it sank. If there's any likelihood of finding a body, an inquest will be ordered, followed by an inquiry into the sinking.'

'If?' asked Shelley. 'You think there is some doubt?'

'You can't tell with wrecks,' said Ryder gently. 'Karel may have been washed overboard before the sinking.'

'But all the time there's a chance of finding a body,' Dirk repeated, 'there's hope. And that means a lifting of the diving ban.'

'Till then we sit around kicking our heels,' muttered Ryder. 'So near and yet so far.'

Shelley experienced a mixture of emotions. The yacht was there! Any day now the ban could be lifted and she would know for sure whether or not the buoyancy tanks were faulty.

'That should stop Joustra's interfering.' Lorraine stood at the sink washing a lettuce. 'To think, I had to go to those lengths before he would do the decent thing and stop the search.' She glanced at Shelley, elbows on the kitchen table, chin in hand. 'What's the matter, dear? You haven't been the same since you went sailing with those ghouls. I knew it would upset you. You shouldn't have gone.'

'Maybe you're right. I'm all mixed up.'

'That's blatantly obvious.' Lorraine's expression softened. 'Do you want to tell me what happened? You can leave out the more intimate details.'

'Nothing happened. It's just that...oh, I don't know. I can't make my feelings out. One minute I want to be with Dirk, the next...' She broke off as the heat invaded her cheeks. 'Why am I so undecided?'

'Because you don't want to be hurt again.' Lorraine leaned back against the cool Delft tiles which lined the kitchen walls. 'You've summed up the kind of man he is, here today and gone tomorrow. Besides being a shady character on the side. A jumped-up scrap-dealer! You're ships that pass in the night and that's the sum total of it. You're attracted to him, of course you are! But an affair would be disastrous for you, because you are capable of loving deeply. For him it would be a pleasant diversion, something to pass the time. That's all.'

Yes, thought Shelley. The first time they had met all her senses had told her to be wary of him.

'Your world fell apart once,' went on Lorraine pensively. 'But you lived to tell the tale. You can't afford to get entangled with a man like that. Casual contacts are not for you. You would end up worse than you started. When you love you give your heart completely. It's a pity you gave it to the wrong man! Your instincts are telling you to steer clear of Joustra. Heed them!'

'You're right!' Shelley straightened her shoulders. 'Thanks, Lorraine. Once more you've helped me put my feelings into perspective. I shall steer clear of him from now on.'

Now she had time to catch her breath, Shelley couldn't understand how she came to be sitting with Dirk in a train speeding northwards.

But he had been so persuasive when he had invited her to spend a long weekend at his home in Friesland she hadn't been inclined to argue. So much for Lorraine's pep talk and her determination to be sensible in future.

The reason for the trip was to collect his own car, which had been undergoing repair, and bring it to Zandvoort. As it was Whit Sunday and there was no chance of the court lifting the diving ban before Tuesday the salvage crew was taking time off.

It hadn't been easy for Shelley to do the same because the holiday season was getting under way. But Greet, surprisingly, had declared that she was bored doing nothing and offered to stand in for her.

That was before she knew why Shelley wanted the break. When she found out she said bitchily, 'You might have told me you were going away for a dirty weekend with Dirk!'

As the crow flies, it was less than a hundred miles to Leeuwarden, the nearest city to Dirk's home, but it seemed much farther. First they had to change trains in Amsterdam, then travel to the herring town of Enkhuizen to cross the IJsselmeer Sea—famous for its eels. During the crossing Dirk told Shelley the story of that stretch of water which she still insisted on calling the Zuyder Zee.

'The bottom is a graveyard for ships, but the same sea bed has provided Holland with thousands of acres of good land, because Dutch engineers have been snipping off a bit here and a bit there for seven centuries.'

She loved to hear him talk, he was so proud of his country.

They boarded another train for the final stage of their journey through fields of black and white Friesian cattle. As always, Shelley was disappointed by the lack of crops, so different from England. The level horizon was dotted with windmills and she saw lakes and canals as straight as rulers stretched across the green landscape.

They had the carriage to themselves and Dirk faced her, perfectly at ease like a great golden cat, its claws sheathed for now, but ready to pounce at any given time.

As she watched he pulled off his tie and loosened the collar of his rust-coloured shirt, then slowly began to turn back the cuffs from his bronzed forearms. She shivered as if an ice cube had slithered down her back.

He grinned suddenly and she saw the flash of his teeth in the sunlight streaming through the windows. She envied the

Dutch their teeth. They were brought up to care for them and she still had to meet the Hollander with more than two fillings.

It was hot and, following his example, she pulled undone the neck of her mint-green safari dress, all pockets and epaulets, letting her thoughts take wing. Was she falling for him? She considered the possibility for a tantalising moment then dismissed it impatiently. Attracted yes, who wouldn't be? But attraction was a world away from love.

All the same...there was something indefinable about her feelings for him. Every time he smiled there was an answering beat of excitement inside her. That was it. He excited her! Why did life play such under-handed tricks? Why did excitement have to come in such impossible packets!

Since meeting him her memories of Ryder had become watered down, but she still remembered the pain. Never again, she reminded herself, would she put her dependence wholly on a man. They couldn't be relied upon.

She closed her eyes, reliving Dirk's caresses, his audacious kisses. He had restored her confidence in herself as a woman but it wouldn't do to set any higher store on it than that.

All at once the train was pulling into Leeuwarden station and Dirk lifted her suitcase from the rack.

'Welcome to Friesland.' He spoke in Dutch but different from the language she was trying to master.

'We speak our own lingo here,' he explained. 'It's more like English than Dutch so you'll pick it up easily. It doesn't go down too well with the rest of Holland, but keeping our identity is important to us.'

He helped her down to the platform, warming to his theme. 'We Frieslanders won our province through courage, hard work and imagination. We battled over the centuries, often alone, against human and natural enemies, so we see every reason to keep our own characteristics and language. You'll find the road signs are in Dutch and Friesland.'

'The Commandant said you were a breed apart,' she murmured.

Her remark pleased him. 'Our origin is obscure. Perhaps we come from Sweden, perhaps we are Celts. When the Romans first came to Holland in about fifty BC we had already been here for three centuries.' He laughed derisively. 'Caesar's legions found the Friesians hard to digest.'

'Tough, eh?'

'You'd better believe it.' He took her arm and guided her towards a taxi rank. 'The early Friesians didn't have it easy. Our number-one enemy was the North Sea. Still is. We were the Marsh Dutch and Homer the Greek referred to our country as the land of eternal fog leading to the gates of Hell, no less. Why, back in ancient times Friesland was described as mud, tidal rivers, salt water, storms and fog. Survival was hard, a never-ending battle, but survive we did!'

She giggled and he sent her a fierce glance.

'Forgive me. I tend to get carried away when I speak of my homeland.' He pointed to a large modern office block. 'Joustra Salvage has its offices on the third floor.'

A group of young women passed them on the pavement, tall bronzed beautiful women with an abundance of fair hair, whose eyes lit up at the sight of Dirk. The greetings came thick and fast and he paused to acknowledge them. Shelley felt more diminutive than ever, a dwarf in a land of giants.

She watched the friendly exchanges and pecks on the cheek. Friesians marry Friesians. Hm, plenty of young Dutch fat stock here. He'd be spoilt for choice when he came to settle down.

'Just neighbours,' he explained, handing her into a taxi. 'We're a close-knit community here.'

They headed north through quaint villages with timbered dwellings and cobbled streets and soon reached rich farming country, the houses set in clusters of trees with huge barns for the cattle. The land was perfectly flat and a boat sailing along a nearby canal seemed to be travelling through fields, its white sail tinted pink in the afternoon sun.

Dirk's home was a splendid Renaissance building reminiscent of a royal lodge, with grey-slated cupolas, neck gables, sunken windows and balanced chimney stacks. It stood in wooded grounds and Shelley glimpsed outbuildings to the rear.

A black-coated manservant opened the door to them. 'We got your message, Master Dirk. Miss Tilda's room has been prepared for the young lady.'

'This is Otto,' said Dirk, clapping the man on the back. 'What you would call an old retainer.'

They followed him into a marble-tiled hall, dominated by an elegant staircase, just as a plump elderly woman came from a side door. She smiled at Dirk then examined Shelley closely.

'And this is Els.' Dirk kissed her wrinkled cheeks. 'The housekeeper and Otto's wife.'

He rapped smartly on an ornate door. 'These are my mother's apartments.'

They entered a cosy sitting-room, cluttered with the usual knick-knacks and occasional furniture.

'*Moeder*, I want you to meet Shelley Pearson.'

His mother offered her hand. '*Mejuffrouw* Pearson.'

Shelley wasn't sure what she had expected. A dignified lady, perhaps, with a sober taste in dress, used to taking tea with the local gentry. She was totally unprepared for the sight of the tall athletic-looking woman clothed in open-necked sports shirt, shorts and trainers. Her pure white hair was held back by a silvery-blue sweat band exactly matching her eyes which contained a keen interest in her son's guest.

'*Moeder*'s into keep-fit,' grinned Dirk. 'She attends the sports centre on Saturday afternoons and jogs every morning. She speaks no English, I'm afraid.'

A tray of lemon tea arrived and Shelley politely answered questions about England, doing the best she could with the language. Familiar with Dutch etiquette, she knew they were a most formal race, not given to using Christian names on short acquaintance, but dignified people who kept their emotions under control and set great store by decorum. That wasn't to say they didn't have a love for the good things of life, but it took time to get to know them. She looked forward to getting to know Mrs Joustra who had a beautiful smile and a voice which overflowed with warmth.

Presently Dirk escorted Shelley upstairs to a bedroom decorated in pink, its windows draped with crisp net, its furniture a hotch-potch of styles. With polished floor, colourful rugs and patchwork-quilted bed, it contained a timeless quality all its own.

Tilda's room.

'It's charming.' She eyed a giant one-eyed teddy bear sitting in an armchair. 'Will I be meeting your sister?'

'No!' he snapped. Then quietly, 'She and Ryder live fifteen miles from here, in Dokkum, but they're spending the weekend in Amsterdam.'

His tone implied he wouldn't have invited Shelley if there had been any chance of her bumping into Ryder's wife!

She touched the top of an old dressing chest worn smooth by the passage of time. 'Does the house belong to you?'

'Yes, my father left it to me.'

There was a beautiful *Stoelklok* with weights, and brackets carved like mermaids. 'It's genuine *Joure*,' said Dirk. 'They don't make them any more, though I believe you can buy reasonably priced replicas. The bell has been removed to stop it chiming all night.' He moved to the door. 'Dinner is at six so you have plenty of time to freshen up.'

After he had gone away, she poked about in the cupboards trying to get a clue as to the character of the room's former occupant. She found two old dolls, a shelf full of schoolgirl novels, a collage of pressed flowers and, on the inside of the wardrobe door, a host of American pop stars' photographs. It was the domain of any normal teenager.

She found a pink-tiled bathroom tucked away under the eaves and took a leisurely bath using the delicately scented essences thoughtfully provided. Then she dressed in a calf-length gown of emerald shantung with a halter neckline, an expensive little number she had bought in the halcyon days before the collapse of Pearson Marine.

Dinner was in a large room overlooking a formal garden. Dirk, appearing immensely attractive in a dark suit, met her at the door and escorted her to an oval table covered with a lace cloth and set with gleaming cutlery, enamelled glassware and silver bowls of flowers.

He stared at the five place settings. 'Who else is coming to dinner, *Moeder?*'

Mrs Joustra smiled. 'Tilda just rang to say she and Ryder have postponed their weekend trip so they can meet your guest.'

As she spoke the door opened and a woman, younger than Shelley, entered walking with the aid of a stick. Pretty, wearing a strawberry-pink trouser suit, her hair a mass of bronze curls about her slim shoulders, she had to be Tilda.

Beside her, giving his support, was Ryder.

Shelley knew she shouldn't stare but

couldn't help it. She wanted to see the woman who had won Ryder's heart and wondered at the girl's motives for wishing to meet her brother's guest. Interest in his activities, or to inspect her husband's former fiancée? Unless she hadn't been given that crumb of information. Knowing Ryder it was possible. Dirk had been kept in the dark.

Dirk kissed the girl's cheeks. 'Tilda! Little *zuster!* You look lovely. When did you get rid of the wheelchair?'

'A couple of months ago,' said Ryder. 'She's making excellent headway since I've been encouraging her to exercise more. She made me swear not to tell you how well she's getting on. She wanted to surprise you.'

'Look, Dirk!' Tilda waved Ryder away and hobbled towards the table. Before she reached it she discarded the stick and took three steps unaided. She collapsed laughing into Ryder's arms and he eased her into her chair.

'Bravo!' exclaimed Dirk delightedly.

He effected the introduction and the two girls shook hands across the table.

'Ryder tells me you are the daughter of Frank Pearson for whom he once worked.'

Tilda's blue eyes were very bright, very shrewd.

She knows, thought Shelley.

She saw Dirk's stricken look, almost pleading with her not to say anything that would connect her more intimately with Ryder.

Shelley recognised the absurdity of the situation. Dirk was tying himself in knots to save Tilda any embarrassment but his anxiety was unnecessary because Tilda knew.

Dutch etiquette being what it was, it would be unthinkable for Tilda to allude to her husband's former engagement while she was in her brother's house. Shelley guessed she would need to watch her tongue if she didn't want to antagonise her host.

CHAPTER 7

The meal was traditional—roll-mop herrings, lamb, milk pudding—but a variety of rich sauces and side dishes transformed each course into a gourmet's delight, while the expertise of the cook was complemented by several bottles of dry Mâcon Supérieur.

They took coffee and liqueurs in a pine-panelled games room dominated by a large pool table. By this time a few neighbours had arrived and the air was soon thick with cigar smoke.

One of the visitors was a distinguished-looking grey-haired man introduced as Dr Boertje. He seemed keen on Mrs Joustra and Shelley was intrigued to witness the intimate glances which passed between them.

'He's a widower,' whispered Dirk. 'Every time I return home I expect to be informed of impending nuptials.'

Tilda was bubbling over with a plan for opening a boutique in Dokkum.

'That's great news,' said Dirk. 'It shows you're taking an interest in life again.'

Tilda slipped her hand in Ryder's as he perched on the arm of her chair. 'It was my handsome husband's idea. I was scared at first but he talked me round.'

'I'll help you get started,' enthused Dirk.

'No, you won't!' Ryder grated out. 'She's doing it on her own.'

The two men stared at each other and Dirk backed down. 'Okay, okay.' His tone conveyed his approval.

They drew lots to play pool and Shelley was knocked out by the doctor in the first round. It was no surprise to her when Ryder won the tournament. He'd invariably beaten her when they'd played in the pub in Tilbury.

'Trust you, Ryder...' she began without thinking. She glanced quickly at Tilda, but the girl was in deep conversation with her mother.

'Watch it!' Dirk hissed in Shelley's ear. She wanted to tell him he was worrying unnecessarily but Otto arrived with a tray of Triple Sec and Dirk called for silence.

'The Friesland toast!' He raised his glass and in a voice brimming with emotion said, 'With five weapons shall we keep our land, with sword and with shield, with spade and with fork and with the spear. Out with the ebb, up with the flood, to fight day and night against the North-kind and the wild Viking, that all Friesians may be free, the born and the unborn, as long as the wind shall blow and the world stands.'

The others chorused 'To Friesland' and drank deeply.

Shelley was moved. As her eyes met

Dirk's a spark seemed to leap between them leaving her weak and breathless.

The Joustra habit was early to bed. The visitors departed. Els moved about collecting coffee cups, glasses, overflowing ashtrays and crushed cigar packets. Otto opened windows to disperse the mingled smells of smoke and spirits. Shelley yawned.

'I'll show you the estate tomorrow,' Dirk promised, escorting her up the stairs.

'That will be nice.'

He opened a door. 'This is my study. Come in for a night cap.' He saw her hesitate. 'Aw, come on!'

Her high heels sank into the thick oatmeal carpet and her eyes appraised a massive oak desk. There were framed photographs of salvage vessels on the chimney breast, adding splashes of colour to the sombre brickwork.

'Hm.' She sat on a couch, the hue of autumn bracken. 'Very masculine.'

Dirk took two glasses from a cabinet and held up a bottle of Triple Sec. 'Okay?'

She nodded and he poured the green liquid.

Sitting beside her he handed her a glass. 'To us.'

There was that intimate look in his eyes again and she gulped the drink down thirstily.

His arms stretched along the back of the couch and his fingers tickled her neck. She affected another yawn.

He eyed the deep vee of her dress. 'Shelley...'

Panic poured over her like treacle on hot toast. 'I'm tired.'

'Your hair fascinates me.' He touched it and waxed lyrical. 'So thick and heavy, like a curtain of dark brown silk shimmering with foxy lights.'

He hooked a finger under her chin and looked at her in a warm, strangely pensive fashion as if absorbing every detail of her face. Her lips trembled and there was a matching awareness in her eyes.

As his head descended she denied that awareness and lifted her mouth to his, knowing she had yearned all evening for this moment and surrendering to the melting sweetness of his kiss.

He moved closer and his mouth grew passionate as it travelled across the smooth creamy skin of her throat and shoulders before claiming her lips again.

No gentle kiss this time and she was

made to know of all his need, all his power. Engulfed by the heady aura of him, an intense shock of pleasure charged to the soles of her feet, like an electric current returning to earth.

He lifted his head to check the effect he was having on her. Then his hand came up to cradle one breast, the warmth of his touch equalling the warmth she had witnessed in his eyes.

She was long past resisting. Too much Triple Sec and wine, she thought crazily, throwing her arms round his neck, her sapphire eyes mirroring the fire he had ignited deep within her.

A clock in the corner of the room began to chime ten o'clock. The sound brought her up with a start.

The spell was broken. What was she doing? Allowing this stranger to touch and fondle her? Hadn't she promised herself never to let a man get this close again?

She got shakily to her feet and bolted across the room. 'It's no good, Dirk. I'm not going to have an affair with you.'

Rough arms caught her before she reached the door and she was propelled into his arms once more. Demanding lips ploughed into hers.

She had no legs to stand on. His kiss was a receding wave dragging the sand from under her. 'Stop it!'

'Shelley, for heaven's sake!' The warm lights in his eyes were extinguished and his tone was loaded with exasperation. 'You can't do this to me.'

'Can't I?' She jerked open the door. 'Goodnight.'

His voice followed her along the corridor. 'You're a mess, Shelley, you know that?'

She stumbled into her room and slammed the door. She shouldn't have come, she thought, turning the key in the lock. It was madness. In her heart of hearts she had known this would happen, known why he had invited her here.

Idiot! she chided herself. She had seen the danger signs and still walked right into the trap. If she were not careful she'd be falling in love with him.

She must leave first thing in the morning.

She woke to the sound of wood pigeons in the trees and the sight of fleecy white clouds in the sky.

Remembering her vow to return to Zandvoort she went down to the kitchen to see if there was a chance of snatching a bite of breakfast without having to go into the dining-room.

Els was stirring something in a large saucepan.

Shelley smiled and gestured towards a plate of bread and butter.

The woman proffered the plate.

'Good morning.' Dirk's deep voice came from behind the open door of the tall fridge and she started as he stepped into view holding a glass of milk. He took a gulp and surveyed her cotton gypsy dress, the colour of forget-me-nots, its neckline caught in a drawstring, its full sleeves gathered at the wrists. 'You look nice and cool.'

Shelley took the mug of strong black coffee Els handed her. 'I'm going back to Zandvoort.'

He pulled out a chair from under the table and she slid into it, placing the plate and mug on the cloth.

She bit into the bread and gazed up at him. His head was dangerously close to the ceiling and his presence dwarfed the room.

He picked up a shiny red apple and sank his strong white teeth into it. 'There are no

135

trains on Sundays.'

The coffee was scalding hot and she hastily put it down. 'I'll take a bus then, hire a car, a bike...'

'Don't be silly,' he murmured. 'I'll drive you back to Zandvoort tomorrow. We're going to church this morning with *Moeder* and the doctor. I'll meet you in the hall in ten minutes.'

She glowered after his retreating back.

The church was decorated with flowers for Whit Sunday and the Joustras had their own pew at the front. Most of the service was unintelligible to Shelley but the enthusiasm of the congregation made up for that. The highlight of the morning was the arrival of the Sunday school children with Whit garlands decorated with birch branches, paper flowers and cones.

Dirk went round with the plate and she suffered a fierce bolt of jealousy as she saw him exchanging smiles with several young women. Her reaction was entirely beyond her reasoning.

They returned to the house for a late lunch then Mrs Joustra went off to change into her tracksuit. She was opening an exhibition of children's athletics that afternoon.

'I'm just the chauffeur,' the doctor told Shelley.

Shelley and Dirk were waving them off when the phone rang. It was Tilda to say there was a *kermis* at Roodkerk and suggesting Dirk and Shelley meet her and Ryder there.

'We have better things to do than go to a fair,' Dirk replied. Replacing the receiver, he said 'I can't get over the change in Tilda. I've got to hand it to Ryder. He's worked wonders.'

'I'm glad.' Shelley stepped out into the sunlight and accompanied him to the rear courtyard where he showed her the former stables, now used as a garage for his silver BMW and his mother's Opel Sports car; and a large kitchen garden.

The air was haunted by an overriding scent of deadnettle and the surrounding trees—magnolia, dogwood and crab-apple — were thick with green leaves.

There was a summerhouse reminiscent of Hansel and Gretel's gingerbread cottage, with a beamed frontage and bay windows. However, on closer inspection, Shelley discovered it was all an illusion. The walls were flat, the architecture merely painted on.

'It's called *trompe-l'oeil,*' said Dirk, seeing her expression of disbelief. He winked. 'Remember, things are not always as they seem.'

'You can say that again!'

The room inside was furnished in the Hinderloopen style with quaintly carved, brightly painted chairs and tables straight from a fairy-tale. Here too the green and vermilion walls had been given the eye-deceiving treatment and there appeared to be dressers with Delft plates and even a long-case clock.

Doubting everything now, Shelley tentatively touched the stove and spinning-wheel, finding them real.

'Tilda and I played here as children,' said Dirk leading her outside where she glimpsed a lake shimmering in the distance.

'It's a large estate.'

'We owned half the area in days gone by. My grandfather was a baron, but titles have no place in modern Holland, apart from the royal family.'

He was standing close enough for her to see the silver flecks in his eyes and she swallowed hard. Spurred by an incomprehensible instinct she placed her hand on his bare arm, toying with the curling blond hair, exploring the sun-bronzed skin, letting the tips of her fingers trace the taut sinews.

He gathered her to him and his eager mouth caught hers. All rational thought was suspended while the fire flared between them, consuming them both.

She set up no opposition when his strong teeth found the drawstring of her neckline and pulled it undone.

Pushing aside the material he dropped his lips to her sensitive skin.

'Oh Dirk!'

He scooped her up and bore her to the chequered shade of the trees, following her gentle descent onto the grass with the full weight of his body.

'Dirkje! Shelley! Where are you?'

It sounded like Tilda's voice, embarrassingly close.

'Hell!' Dirk rolled away and stood up. 'My sister has perfect timing, has she not?'

He took Shelley's hand and hauled her to her feet.

She smoothed her hair and tidied her neckline as Tilda and Ryder came through the trees.

'There you are!' Tilda leaned heavily on Ryder's arm. 'Why didn't you answer?'

Ryder darted a shrewd glance at Shelley and Dirk, and his eyes darkened perceptively. 'Perhaps they didn't wish to be disturbed.'

'Oh!' Tilda gave a delightful little laugh. 'Is that right? I'm sorry, Dirkje.'

'What do you want?' Dirk asked ungraciously.

'We've come to take you to the fair.'

Dirk shrugged helplessly. 'Why not?'

They went in Ryder's car. As they paused at a level crossing for a train to roar past, Shelley said, 'You told me there were no trains today.'

'I lied,' Dirk replied blithely.

Roodkerk was bustling with activity and long before they reached the market square they could hear the music of the fair. There were the usual rides and games of skill and Shelley breathed in the aroma of raw herrings, humbugs and *poffertjes*. Dirk purchased a bagful of these small fritters and passed them round.

As Shelley wiped her sugary fingers on her handkerchief she saw Dirk watching her with a wry smile and she blushed, acknowledging how close she had come to surrendering to her instincts. But was an affair what she wanted? She was certain that's all it would be. She should be grateful to Tilda and yet...she felt deprived. Oh, why was life so difficult?

Dirk tried his luck on the sideshows and soon she was cradling a toy panda, a water pistol, a china dog and a coconut. And all the time they touched—as he lifted her into a chairoplane, dragged her out of a dodgem-car, helped her down the steps of the carousel.

Dirk was concerned for Tilda. 'You mustn't overdo it, love.'

'Stop fussing. I'm fine.'

They dined in a restaurant in the square and afterwards the two women went to the power-room together—much to Dirk's dismay.

'Poor Dirk.' Tilda checked her hair in the mirror. 'He's so protective. He won't accept I'm a big girl now.'

Shelley remained silent, sensing what was to come.

'I've known all along about you and Ryder,' Tilda confided. 'But we decided against telling Dirk. He was so set against my marrying a non-Friesian we didn't want to give him any more ammunition. Of course he's met you now and will have discovered the truth for himself. I suppose I'll have to confess to him soon that I know.'

So brother and sister had been protecting each other.

'I was prepared to dislike you,' Tilda admitted, 'but you're nice and I can't. I feel pity for you. Ryder told me everything.'

Everything? Did that include the lies and the betrayal? She guessed not.

'Don't worry, Shelley, I'm not the jealous type. Ryder's past is no concern of mine. But I wanted us to have this talk, to clear the air. If you're going to be seeing a lot of Dirk then we're bound to meet and I didn't want any bad feeling.'

Shelley warmed to this girl who was wise beyond her years. She plainly loved Ryder and Shelley sincerely hoped she wouldn't live to regret it. Ryder was easy to love—and difficult to hate. Even now Shelley had to work hard at it. A cold shiver assailed her, strengthening her resolve to leave Friesland heartwhole.

'I don't think I'll be seeing a lot of Dirk.'

'Oh, forgive me.' Tilda looked flustered. 'I thought...'

They spent the rest of the evening at a marionette show and the moon was high when Ryder dropped them back at the house.

As she watched the car speed away, a surge of sheer fright charged Shelley's body. It was late. Mrs Joustra would have gone to bed. The servants too.

Dirk took her hand and pushed open the door as the sound of laughter floated to their ears.

'What the...?' Dirk frowned.

The hall lanterns were dimmed but there was a streak of light shining under the games room door. All at once it opened and Mrs Joustra came out.

'Come on in, Dirk. And you too, Shelley. The Velts have called to see us. Come and say hello to them.'

'Great!' muttered Dirk.

Shelley hung back. 'I won't if you don't mind. I'm rather tired.'

She ignored Dirk's look of pleading and sped up the stairs. It had been another narrow squeak. She knew very well what was on Dirk's mind and didn't think she would have had the strength to resist him again. Now she was safe. Tomorrow she would return to Zandvoort still in one piece.

She put on silk pyjamas and brushed her hair. It had been a day of changing moods and her mind was all topsy-turvy. But casual involvements were not for her. It was best this way.

Presently she sensed Dirk outside her door, saw the handle turn, heard him softly call her name. She held her breath and he went away.

Her initial relief was succeeded by despair and the feeling of self-deception was very real. Who was she kidding? Her eyes in the mirror glimmered like bright jewels and her heightened colour gave her a dewy glow. What she saw was a woman in love.

So that was it? She'd fallen for a tall rugged guy who could only mean heartache and trouble. She wasn't ready to get on that old treadmill again. Ryder had accepted her love, destroyed it and thrown it back in her face. Now she had come close to committing herself to a man who asked much more of her than Ryder had even realised existed. One could cross off a man like Ryder, walk away and start a new life—she'd done it. But there would be no easy way to walk away from Dirk. She knew it as surely as she knew the sun would rise.

She woke early. The birds were barely up and night still lingered in the trees outside.

She washed, did her exercises and reached for a bottle of hand lotion, only to find the screw-top lid was on a cross-thread. 'Darn it!' she muttered as it refused to budge. She doubted if anyone would be about yet but Mrs Joustra might be jogging in the grounds.

She pulled on her paisley robe, dropped the bottle into the pocket and went onto the balcony that ran the length of the house. The gardens below were deserted and a wraithlike mist hung over the lawns.

She walked along the balcony to where light streamed from an uncurtained window. Gazing in she saw a wide bed with a biscuit-coloured cover, a dark brown carpet, an array of men's toiletries on the dressing chest, a crumpled linen suit flung carelessly over the back of a chair.

She stood there transfixed, as in a dream.

The room was unoccupied, but a cloud

of steam came from a door at the far end. In a moment Dirk came through that door applying a towel to his wet hair.

His unclothed manliness had a weakening effect on her senses and she was unable to tear her eyes away from him.

He looked up and saw her. Making no attempt to hide his nakedness, he crossed to open the window and beckon her through. She went as if pulled by strings.

She continued to stare, hypnotised by his nearness. When he spread his arms invitingly, she rushed into them. They closed round her and she felt his immediate need. There came an answering call from the nucleus of her womanhood.

He removed her robe and his hands rambled over the silky texture of her pyjamas, seeking the fastenings. As his fingers slipped from button to button she whimpered. Why was he taking so long?

At last the garments slid to a heap around her feet. He caressed her, his hand closing on one swollen breast. She gave a cry of delight.

His hard mouth followed the same sensitive path his hands had pioneered, teasing her to a new plateau of desire.

'Shelley, *lieveling.*'

For a split second her mind cleared long enough for her to think about the outcome. Would it mean the same to him as it meant to her? And what did it mean to her? Too many questions! Every cell cried out for him and this wanting had to be taken care of. Now.

In another moment she was lying beneath him on the soft coverlet. As she lifted her mouth to his, she felt the heat of his blood, the sure flame in him, till her own blood tingled and her senses danced.

Somewhere outside a bird began the dawn chorus. It was the last thing she heard as she clung to the man who was the source of—and the only shelter from—the tornado raging about her.

CHAPTER 8

As their bodies descended from the heights, she lay with her head on his chest listening to the thud of his heartbeat.

'*Lieveling!*'

'I love you, Dirk, *Ik houd van jou.*'

Caressing his lips, his face, the heavy fringe of golden hair, the scar that ran across his cheek, she willed him to reciprocate.

He remained silent and she acknowledged that love and sex didn't necessarily go hand in hand for men. She mustn't expect too much.

His kiss, tender yet ardent, conveyed to her what his lips could not say and her spirits soared. Dutchmen were reticent in showing their emotions, but give him time!

Later, as she walked back to her own room, she buried her hands in her pockets and located the bottle of lotion. Taking it out she automatically tried the cap once more and it opened easily.

She laughed. How very Freudian!

They breakfasted together on the creeper-covered terrace, helping each other to toast and *hagelslag* and orange juice and coffee, while exchanging secret smiles.

Afterwards they walked hand in hand and whispering endearments among the rhododendrons. Shelley felt marvellous.

Later as she waited for Dirk to bring the BMW round, Ryder bounded through the front door. 'Hi! I came over to pick up a book... Say, you look terrific!'

She smiled. The cherry-red flying suit, its collar turned up, its waist nipped in by a webbing belt, its sleeves pushed past her elbows, exactly matched her mood. 'Thanks.'

He held his head on one side. 'You're different somehow, you're glowing.' He let out a low whistle. 'I get it! You little fool! God! You certainly know how to pick your men.'

'Be quiet!'

'Don't you see? He's only interested in keeping you away from me?' His lips curled contemptuously. 'He's so riddled with guilt he'd do anything to save his sister embarrassment and pain. Why do you think he stomachs me?'

'Shut up!' She grabbed her case as a horn sounded outside. 'Stop behaving like a jealous lover.'

She went down the steps towards the silver car, her thoughts a ragbag of uncertainties. In the dark attic of her mind was Dirk's offer, made on the night of the bad moon rising. 'If you want a bit of fun, have it with me'.

During the drive to Zandvoort, Ryder's taunts lay heavily on Shelley's heart. What better way for Dirk to keep her and Ryder apart than to make love to her himself?

'You're very quiet,' Dirk broke into her thoughts. 'You belong to me now, *lieveling*. No looking at other men. No looking at Ryder.'

Under the circumstances it was the worst remark he could have made. All at once she felt as brittle as glass. One touch could break her in two, shatter her in a million pieces.

'You're not regretting this morning?'

Was she? Her motives were straightforward enough. She loved him. But what about his motives? She thought again of his love-making, his tenderness and his passion. Had she been mistaken in thinking his behaviour spelt out his love for her? She'd been mistaken before.

She set her doubts aside. Sooner or later she had to learn to take people at face value, learn to trust again, starting with Dirk.

'No I'm not regretting anything.'

They reached the hotel just before eight to find the Commandant in an uncharacteristic state of panic.

'Thank goodness you're back, Shelley,'

he cried. 'We've had a rush of visitors and now the cocktail waiter's gone down with measles. Can you do the night-shift, from now till seven in the morning?'

She hesitated and he went on. 'You owe me a favour for letting you off for the weekend. Your stand-in was hopeless and I told her so.'

Poor Greet, thought Shelley. 'All right.'

'Hell!' said Dirk when they were alone again. 'I had plans for tonight. I might as well get my head down. I want to get up early tomorrow to go to the courthouse.'

Shelley was put to work in the bar where Greet was talking with a group of noisy guests.

'Hi, Shelley!' The Dutchwoman wore a white dress of silk noil which highlighted her magnificent hair. 'Nice weekend?' Her words were slurred and she had obviously had more than her limit of *Parfait Amour*.

'I'd rather not talk about it.'

Greet brightened as she came to the wrong conclusion. 'Guess Dirk is one frustrated male.'

Shelley was tired and made several mistakes mixing the cocktails; added someone's bill incorrectly and spilt a glass of advocaat over the carpet.

151

At three o'clock the Commandant told her to go home.

'You're no good to me in this state.'

She apologised and looked about to see if Greet needed any help in getting back home, but she had disappeared.

Shelley went along the corridor and thought of Dirk in his lonely bed upstairs. She savoured the ecstasy of his love-making, the way he had excited her almost beyond endurance. Her body was still on fire for his touch and there was an ache deep inside her that recent experience told her only he could make go away. Damn it, she loved him—and she wanted him!

In the foyer, old Popken sprawled across the desk, snoring loudly. She crept past him and lifted down the key to Dirk's suite then took the elevator to the fourth floor. All was quiet as she unlocked the door. She stealthily crossed the sitting-room and went through to the bedroom.

It glowed with an eerie blueness as the bright moon, in its last quarter, shone through the net curtains billowing in the gentle breeze from the open window.

Her ears detected the sound of steady breathing and she made out a form in the bed.

As she tiptoed over the carpet something caught her eye and she looked quickly towards the armchair, saw the movement of a hand.

Dirk, clothed in a loose black robe, sat in profile to her, gazing out into the night. The moonlight turned his hair to silver and etched his gaunt cheeks so that he resembled a Greek statue. The sight brought an involuntary sigh to her lips.

He started at the sound and turned his head, a shocked look befalling his features. 'Shelley! What the...!' His voice was no more than a strangled whisper as he leapt to his feet.

With a sickening premonition she swung back to the shape under the bed-sheet and her heart took a dive.

The woman lay face down but there was no mistaking that cloud of ginger hair fanned out over the pillows. The sheet barely covered Greet's naked body and one arm was flung out as if to embrace the empty space beside her. The white silk dress lay crumpled on the floor along with various items of underwear and a pair of high heels.

Shelley reeled back and gave a low cry like an animal in pain.

'Shelley!' Dirk came towards her, hands outstretched, a look of pleading on his face.

She jerked away from him and burst into tears, hot scalding tears that burned her cheeks. She tasted their salt.

'Shelley, *lieveling,* I know it looks bad, but it's not what you're thinking.' He tried to take her in his arms but she evaded him.

'Leave me alone,' she hissed, wiping at her cheeks with her hands and staring at him through a misty veil. 'How many women do you need, for heaven's sake?'

'If you'll only listen...'

He had raised his voice and Greet stirred. 'What's going on?' she asked in Dutch, her words muffled by the pillows. 'Dirk, honey, come back to bed.'

Shelley stumbled blindly out of the room. She heard Dirk call after her and rushed headlong down the stairs, her heart hammering in her chest.

On the bottom step she paused, listening for sounds of pursuit. She heard voices on the top floor as if someone was complaining about the noise, and let herself out of the side door.

At the bungalow she took sanctuary in

her bedroom and turned on all the lights. Darkness was the enemy, making her prey to the sensations of betrayal that racked her body. Despite the warm night she was shivering.

Without knowing what she was doing, she dragged herself into the bathroom, filled the tub and immersed herself up to her neck in the soothing water.

Her nerves were threadbare and her heart seemed to have been torn out by the roots. Over and over, like a record stuck in the groove, her brain replayed the words, 'Come back to bed, honey. Come *back* to bed.'

History had repeated itself. She had given her love and trust and been cheated in return. Oh how could he? 'Dirk, honey, come *back* to bed.'

The water cooled. As she let it out, it was like pulling the plug on any feeling she had for him. Her love had changed to hate. She wouldn't be so foolish again.

'You look ghastly,' said Greet, glancing up from the breakfast table as Shelley made her listless entrance. 'How strange! I over imbibe and you get the hangover.'

Shelley swallowed a temptation to hit

back. What good would a row do? Greet obviously knew nothing of her presence in Dirk's room last night. They were both victims.

Lorraine, hair tousled, eyes dark-ringed, came in and caught the tail-end of her daughter's remark. 'I wish you wouldn't drink so much, Greet. And where did you get to last night?'

'I was amusing myself, if you must know.'

Shelley's heart gave a sickening lurch, and she choked on her coffee.

'Goodness! What's up with everybody today?' asked Greet. 'You look like a pair of zombies. It's not at all like you, mother. I suppose you're worrying about the court hearing.'

'A little. The judge is a stranger to me. I was hoping for *Mijnheer* Heusden, but he's ill. His stand-in is a much younger man.'

Later Shelley, dressed in old tee-shirt and jeans, her hair caught back in a pony-tail went to tackle the weeds in the front garden. It was there Dirk found her.

'Go away!' she snapped, brandishing the hoe.

'Shelley.' He gripped her wrist. 'You must listen.'

She gave a vain tug. 'There's nothing you can say.'

'There's plenty.' He wrestled the hoe from her and threw it down. 'I can explain if you'll let me.'

She looked away, not wishing to see the face she had loved, the mouth she had kissed, contorted with lies.

'Remember the gingerbread cottage?' he asked. 'The *trompe-l'oeil?* Things are not always as they seem...'

'I'm not listening.'

He gave her a little shake. 'When someone tapped on my door last night I thought it was you. I soon found my mistake. Greet was drunk and started making a nuisance of herself so I let her sleep it off.' He added deliberately, 'I never laid a hand on her. I sat in the chair.'

She succeeded in wrenching herself free and clamped her hands over her ears. 'Shut up! I won't listen. You're not making a fool of me again.'

He pulled her hands down. 'You said you loved me.'

'Love!' she screamed. 'What do I know about love?'

He shook his head sadly. 'Ryder did more damage than I thought.'

She drew a sharp breath. 'Leave Ryder out of it. His betrayal can't compare with yours. You took me to your home with the express purpose of making love to me.'

'I can't deny it.'

'You planned it solely to keep me away from Ryder,' she accused him and, wanting to inflict punishment on him for her humiliation, added 'Because of Tilda's accident.' She drove the message home. 'Because you feel responsible for it!'

His face darkened and she knew her barb had found its mark. He let her go. 'Okay, if that's what you want to think, go ahead.' His expression grew arrogant. 'Yes, that was my motive entirely, to keep you away from Ryder.'

There! She had the condemning admission from his own lips and she went cold.

'Shelley...'

'Just go away! I hate you!'

He flinched then pivoted on his heel and strode away.

Angry tears stung her eyes. She was furious with herself for allowing her heart to override her head—again. In spite of vowing not to expect too much she had expected everything.

The days that followed were the unhappiest in her life—and that included her post-Ryder period. With so many blond giants around she fancied she saw Dirk's face in every crowd. She was in that wilderness again, but this time there seemed to be no escape.

The court ban was lifted two days later and the salvage crew was free to resume the search for the diamonds. Lorraine was distraught.

'They won't be diving straight away,' Shelley offered her a crumb of comfort. 'Ryder is still in Friesland and Henk is in Limburg with his fiancée. The girl on the switchboard told me messages have been sent to both requesting their return. Until they arrive Dirk won't dive alone.'

She was wrong, however. The Commandant told her that Dirk had tired of hanging about and was taking the matter into his own hands.

By the end of the day the hotel was buzzing with the results of Dirk's investigation. A badly-decomposed body, presumably Karel's, was in the wreck, but the water-tight compartment, supposed to have contained the diamonds, was empty!

Lorraine locked herself in Karel's study and refused to come out. In the end Greet discovered a duplicate key in the bureau drawer and led her mother to bed.

Ryder and Henk arrived and the three salvage men sat huddled in the corner of the hotel lounge discussing the situation in low tones.

The following morning Ryder sought Shelley out.

'The plot thickens!' He watched her folding table-napkins into water-lily shapes. 'Curiouser and curiouser. But did the lady know the score?'

Shelley grimaced at his string of clichés. 'Which lady?'

'The lady witch, Lorraine van Hoorn.'

'Must you talk in riddles?'

'Sorry!' His handsome face was wreathed in a knowing smile. 'What no diamonds!'

'You knew all along that was a chance you had to take. Dirk should have accepted Lorraine's offer.'

'What offer?' His topaz eyes were keen with interest.

'Oh! Didn't he tell you? She offered to compensate you for your trouble if you went away.'

'The woman sounds as if she's got something to hide.'

'But this clears her surely. Finding the body proves Karel didn't abscond with the loot.'

'Somebody did.'

Shelley frowned. 'Ye-es.'

'Why didn't she want the body found, if it clears her?'

'It wasn't that she didn't want the body found. She didn't want the grave disturbed.'

'Even if it cleared her name and her husband's?'

Yes, it was mystifying, but Lorraine had been under a strain and couldn't be blamed for wanting to keep Karel's last resting place sacrosanct.

'Well, it'll be disturbed now,' said Ryder. 'The judge ruled it isn't an official grave and there will have to be a proper funeral. An inquest too, I should think.'

'Poor Lorraine! She'll be so upset.' Shelley hesitated. 'I suppose the yacht will be brought up too? We'll find out once and for all...'

'Yes, my dear. We'll find out once and for all what made it sink.'

Shelley took Bello for a long walk over the dunes. As the dog ran free she gazed out over the shifting sea and tried to work out her feelings.

That morning, following a dive by a police frogman, Dirk had been arrested for stealing a million pounds' worth of uncut diamonds from the wreck of the *Angela Rose*.

It had come as a shock to her and she still couldn't believe he was a thief. And yet, what did she know of him? Could he be short of money? The upkeep of his home must be considerable to say nothing of those offices. Supposing Joustra Salvage wasn't doing so well after all, she mused, recalling how her father had bluffed his way out of situations in the past.

She heard someone approaching and was surprised to see Dirk striding towards her. His expression was drawn and he needed a shave.

'I thought you were locked up,' she greeted him coolly.

He patted the dog. 'I'm out on bail.'

'What do you want?'

'Your help.'

Her laugh was loaded with irony.

He ran his eyes over her simple cotton

dress. 'I haven't time to mess about. This is a bad business. Joustra Salvage could go under.'

'What's that to do with me?'

'I know you consider I'm a first-class swine but think what it will do to Tilda if her brother is branded a thief. And if the outfit folds Ryder would be out of a job for a start. If you won't help for my sake, do it for Tilda.'

'That's below the belt. Have you no conscience...?'

'Be quiet!' He stared at her and demanded bluntly, 'Do you think I stole the gems?'

She made up her mind. 'No.'

'Thank you.' He gave a tight smile. 'I know I didn't take them, so that only leaves Lorraine van Hoorn.'

Shelley's head was spinning. 'You've lost me.'

'I want to search the bungalow. That shrine room you mentioned seems a good place to start. She keeps it locked, I imagine?'

Shelley jutted her jaw. 'I won't do it.'

He went on imperviously. 'I want you to wait till both Lorraine and Greet are expected to be away for some time, then call me over and we'll go through the place together to see what we can find.'

'No...' She was wavering.

He grinned. 'Please, Shelley. For Tilda. Then I'll get out of your life for good—if that's what you want!'

'Oh it is!'

'Then you'll help me?'

'I suppose so.'

Her opportunity came a week later when Greet drove her mother into Haarlem for an exhibition of sculpture for which Lorraine had entered a statuette of Greet.

Dirk arrived in answer to Shelley's phone call, accompanied by a tall young man with a drooping moustache.

'This is Piet,' said Dirk. 'One of the local cops, incognito. I thought it best to have a witness. I don't want to be accused of planting the diamonds here myself.'

'What a devious mind you have.' Shelley quickly ushered them in. 'You're wasting your time, you know.'

She produced the spare key that Greet had found and unlocked the study door. 'Promise me you won't damage anything and you'll leave it all as you find it.'

The two men nodded routinely and

began their search, examining the drawers and cupboards first. When that produced a negative result they felt the linings of Karel's coat and cap, then moved on to tap the walls for hidden recesses. 'We'll roll back the carpets and take up every floorboard if necessary,' Dirk promised. 'If we don't find anything today we'll come back again and again until we've searched the whole house.'

Shelley heaved a sigh. 'Must you?'

He was staring at the bust of Karel standing on a plinth in the window. 'What do you reckon, Piet?'

The policeman produced a penknife and turned the bust upside down.

Shelley sprang forward. 'Oh, please be careful!' She tried to take the bust but it was heavier than she expected and it slid from her hands. Dirk made a grab for it but missed.

For a moment they all three performed an animated conjuring act to save it, but it eluded them and crashed onto the desk. The pieces flew in all directions and there was a great shower of what looked like water droplets, caught in prisms of sunshine streaming through the window, and shimmering with all the colours of the rainbow. Then came a steady pit-a-pat as they hit the floor.

Shelley, dazed and excited by what she saw, was to relive that moment over and over again in slow motion.

She came to the conclusion that only a million pounds' worth of diamonds could sparkle like that.

CHAPTER 9

'How's your godmother?' asked Ryder ambling over the courtyard to where Shelley was washing down the Citroën. 'I hear the Commandant put up the bail for her. Has she said anything?'

'Not a lot. She was hurt that I'd let Dirk search the study, but she doesn't blame me. She says I was led astray by his cunning. I still don't know why I did it.' She wrung out the wash-leather. 'Do you really think Lorraine stole the diamonds and hid them in the bust?'

'Yes.'

'But how did she get them? They were on the sea bed.'

He raised one eyebrow. 'Were they?'

'Weren't they?'

'Haven't you wondered why she didn't want the boat disturbed?'

She shook her head in bewilderment. 'I can't think straight any more.'

'Poor Shelley.' He put his hand under her chin. 'Your nice world doesn't recognise crookery among friends. But it'll all be straightened out soon. I've just heard they're sending down government divers to the *Angela Rose*. Then there'll be an inquest on Karel and an inquiry into the sinking. We'll get the truth at last.' He raked his fingers through his luxuriant brown hair. 'Or will we?'

'Must you always be so cryptic?'

'You'll miss me when I'm gone.' He laughed gently. 'Yes, we're leaving tomorrow.'

'Leaving?' she echoed. Dirk was leaving, going out of her life. She would never see him again. Tears pricked her eyes and she blinked rapidly in an effort to dispel them.

'My dear!' Ryder looked concerned. 'Is it Dirk? Well, don't say I didn't warn you.'

'Yes, you warned me.'

He put a comforting arm about her and gave her his handkerchief. 'Here. All that black stuff's running.'

She dabbed at her cheeks. 'It all seems so hopeless...life...'

'Goes on!' he insisted.

She stared at the black smudges on the white linen. 'I'm sorry.'

'Look, go and wash your face and I'll take you out to dinner, shall I? Somewhere trendy.'

She sniffed. 'Yes, I'd like that. Thanks.'

She chose a shimmery silver evening top and long white skirt, pencil slim. The mirror told her she looked good with no evidence of the turmoil raging within her.

He took her to *De Uitzichttoren*—a very smart restaurant at the top of a sixty-metre tower with a view of the town's illuminations.

She was glad she'd come. The food and wine were excellent and Ryder was a scintillating companion. His witty conversation kept her from feeling too sorry for herself.

Both were laughing as they tumbled out of the taxi in front of the Hotel Klokken. In tight skirt and high heels, Shelley was forced to cling to Ryder's arm as she manoeuvred the cobbled forecourt. They had reached the steps when Dirk's BMW pulled up beside them and he and Greet alighted.

Shelley's heart sank at the sight of them. It looked as though Greet was still 'amusing' herself with Dirk.

As all four of them were bathed in the light streaming from the foyer, Dirk's eyes smouldered with anger.

'This looks very cosy, Ryder. Been somewhere nice?' His voice was saw-edged. 'What the eye doesn't see, eh?'

Ryder grinned easily. 'All quite innocent.'

'It looks like it!' Dirk's heated gaze washed over Shelley's dressy outfit then swung back to Ryder. 'Don't your marriage vows mean anything to you?'

'Now wait a minute...' Ryder's expression hardened.

'No, you wait a minute!' Dirk's fist shot out and caught Ryder's jaw a glancing blow that sent him staggering.

Shelley gave a squeal of alarm.

'What the...!' exclaimed Ryder, recovering his balance. 'Why the histrionics?'

'You're a married man!' snapped Dirk.

'Oh, is that what this is all about?'

169

Ryder enquired dryly. 'You could have fooled me.'

Greet intervened. 'Come on, Dirk. Buy me a drink.'

He breathed heavily for a few moments then sent such a venomous glance at Shelley, she recoiled from its impact.

He turned abruptly, mounted the steps two at a time and disappeared into the foyer.

Greet shrugged at Ryder. 'Well, it couldn't be clearer than that.' And she followed Dirk at a leisurely pace.

Shelley was stunned by the events of the past few minutes and couldn't begin to understand Greet's meaning. 'Ryder, are you all right?'

'Sure.' He fingered his jaw. 'Nothing broken.'

'I feel responsible. If you hadn't taken me out...'

'Forget it!' He straightened his tie. 'He can't be blamed, the poor sap, it comes to all of us in the end.'

'Huh? What are you talking about now?'

'Never you mind.'

'You don't think he'll tell Tilda?'

'Not a chance.' Ryder gave her a sideways look. 'Dear sweet Shelley, my marriage was not the issue here.'

'I don't understand.'

'No, dear, I can see you don't.' He proffered his arm. 'I think I'll leave it that way.'

Lorraine bore up well during the inquest on Karel's death. Supported by Shelley and Greet, she gave her evidence in clear even tones, telling the court how her husband had phoned her from London prior to starting out on his fateful journey.

She was spared having to identify the remains because they were unrecognisable. Identity was confirmed by a Smith-Petersen pin inserted in his thigh after he broke the neck of his femur in a road accident—the reason for his limp.

The government frogman told the coroner he had discovered the body in the hold of the yacht. Karel's clothing had disintegrated but an engraved antique bottle, known to have contained tablets for a heart condition, lay nearby, its cap removed and the contents washed away.

The van Hoorns' family doctor confirmed that Karel had suffered a mild coronary a month before the accident.

Shelley stole a glance at Lorraine whose

expression revealed she had known about the state of Karel's health.

'Poor Papa,' said Greet. 'Why didn't you tell me?'

'He didn't want you to know,' her mother replied.

Dirk had sent a statement describing his discovery of the remains during his solo dive from the salvage vessel. Shelley felt an ache of disappointment as she listened, having secretly hoped he would attend the inquest in person.

The court deliberated for a while but there was no clear verdict. The cap-less bottle indicated Karel had suffered a heart attack and may have been in the act of taking a tablet when he was drowned as the boat sank and the water rushed in. Death could have been due to the heart attack or the drowning. It was all speculation, but either way the evidence was damning for Frank Pearson.

All the way home Shelley thought about her father and could hardly believe her eyes when, on arriving at the bungalow, she saw him standing on the porch.

She hurled herself into his arms, a little girl again. 'Daddy! Oh, Daddy! Thank goodness you've come!'

Worry and a sense of failure had taken their toll of Frank Pearson and he appeared older than his fifty-five years. A wiry man of average height, his skeletal cheeks were darkly tanned after working in Saudi Arabia, while his thick hair, once the same colour as Shelley's, and his moustache were iron-grey.

He gave her a bear hug. 'I've been reading about the goings on in Zandvoort and reckoned I had to see for myself. Unfortunately my plane was late so I missed the inquest.' His eyes wandered to Lorraine and he smiled warmly.

'Frank!' Her face was radiant. 'This is the nicest surprise I've had in months. After this business today I was beginning to think the good times were past for me.'

He gathered her into his arms, delivering two loud kisses to her cheeks. 'My dear Lorraine. It's wonderful to see you again.'

Shelley rustled up a light meal and they talked non-stop, leaving alone the subject uppermost in their minds—the death of Karel. His ghost haunted the room.

As Greet cleared away, Frank said, 'Will someone please tell me the result of the inquest. I've got to know.'

Lorraine was overcome by a fit of

sobbing. Frank held her hand while Shelley filled him in about the inquest.

'Looks like I had it all wrong,' he remarked solemnly. 'I don't know how it happened, Lorraine, but can you ever forgive me for causing Karel's death?'

'It was an accident,' said Greet. 'A heart attack most likely. We must wait for the inquiry into the sinking.'

Frank stared into Lorraine's chalky face. 'You should be in bed.' He handed her over to Greet. 'Look after your mother. We'll talk again in the morning.'

'Yes, I am tired,' Lorraine admitted. 'You're welcome to sleep on the sofa. Shelley will find you some bedding.'

'Much obliged.'

When they were alone, Frank said, 'Lorraine seems devastated.'

'She's on bail for robbery, you know.' Shelley poured him another cup of coffee. 'What I can't understand is, how did she get hold of the diamonds?'

Frank pursed his lips. 'Karel must have got them to her somehow, before the yacht sank.'

'So she is involved!'

'It seems so.' He smiled suddenly. 'And what have you been doing with yourself?

174

Your last letter mentioned a guy called Dirk.'

She turned her face away to hide the anguish. 'He's gone away.'

'I see.' Frank was silent for a while. 'So we're both on the loose. We'll have to talk about the future. You can do better than dogsbodying and I don't want to go back to Saudi Arabia.'

'You mean...go to England? But I wanted to stay for the inquiry...' How could she leave? All the while she remained in Zandvoort Dirk knew where to find her.

'Not necessarily.' Frank seemed to understand better than she gave him credit for. 'There are possibilities here. Besides I haven't seen Lorraine for ages and we've got a lot to catch up on...if she can bear to speak to me after what I'm guilty of.'

Shelley recalled Lorraine's delight at seeing Frank again. He seemed the one ray of light on her horizon.

The inquiry was set for the end of July and the day dawned overcast. The subject had caught the public's imagination and the room was packed. What better way to spend a dull afternoon?

175

Lorraine had been withdrawn the past few weeks and only came alive when she was with Frank.

'Don't worry,' he told her. 'It's just routine.'

It was far from routine!

The drama began almost at once. The expert working on the recovered wreck had found holes in both buoyancy tanks and another in the bottom of the boat under the engine. When pressed he declared that in no way could these holes have been made accidentally or caused by striking a log.

Uproar reigned as Lorraine moaned and slid to the floor in a faint, and flashbulbs burst as cameramen rushed up to get their photographs.

The inquiry was halted for ten minutes while Lorraine recovered and when they proceeded Shelley could feel the tension of all concerned, her father particularly as he leaned forward to catch every word.

The expert was asked to explain how, in his opinion, the holes were caused.

'Deliberately. With an axe, most likely.'

Lorraine gasped and Frank put his arm round her as a look of understanding crossed his face. The glance he tossed at Shelley was triumphant and she dared to hope.

'In my opinion,' went on the expert, 'Karel van Hoorn made those holes in the buoyancy tanks then went below to axe another hole underneath the engine.'

'It's a lie!' Lorraine was on her feet shouting hysterically. 'That is conjecture. Why should my husband want to do such a thing? How dare you say he deliberately sank the yacht? You're blackening his name. He's dead and can't answer back, but I'll sue you for every cent you have. I'll...'

She collapsed sobbing and the inquiry was postponed.

Lorraine was quiet all evening, but as Shelley handed round mugs of coffee, she said plaintively, 'Oh Frank, what tangled webs we weave!'

He watched her kindly and Shelley had the impression he had been waiting for this moment. 'Would you like to tell me about it, my dear?'

'I've wanted to tell you,' she replied. 'I've hated deceiving everyone, you most of all. As you must have guessed, it was planned from the start. Karel would sink the yacht and steal the diamonds.'

The words made Shelley's scalp go cold.

Lorraine cradled her mug in her hands. 'Only I didn't know it was going to be your yacht, Frank, I swear. I thought he planned to sink his own yacht the *Brugman II*. It was only when I rendezvoused with him at sea that I discovered he was sailing the *Angela Rose.*'

'How about starting from the beginning,' suggested Frank. 'Karel came to me that day asking if I would lend him my yacht because his had broken down.'

'Had it broken down? Did you check?'

'Yes, I offered to repair it for him but he said it would take too long.'

'He must have immobilised it then.' Lorraine leaned her head back against the chair. 'I'd believe anything now. But the plan was to sail the *Brugman II* from London, going through Customs in the normal way to prove he had the diamonds on board.'

'That's right,' Frank interposed. 'After I'd shown him the modifications of the yacht I saw the Customs men go aboard. I've been over that night a thousand times.'

'Me too!' Slowly, painfully, Lorraine told them how, disguised in a blonde wig and using a false name, she had hired a motor launch from further up the coast then rendezvoused with Karel six miles out from Zandvoort. There was never much shipping in that area, it was why he had chosen it. She had been shocked to see the *Angela Rose* and asked why he had changed his plans, but he refused to enlighten her. He had taken the sealed box containing the gems from the water-tight compartment and passed them to her on a hooked pole, saying he'd see her the following day. She returned the launch to the hire firm and went back to Zandvoort to wait for Karel.

He planned to sink the yacht after sending out a radio message to the effect that he had hit a log and was taking on water fast. Before the boat sank he would inflate the life-raft and row ashore, but would 'get into difficulties' when he was in sight of the coastguard station and send up a maroon for assistance. He knew that the moment he stepped ashore he would be subjected to a Customs search. With his rescuers as witnesses, it would be proved emphatically that he did not have the diamonds with him and they would be presumed to be at the bottom of the sea.

Frank expelled his breath slowly. 'It was a brilliant idea. It might have worked too.'

Lorraine closed her eyes. 'But as we all know, he never made it. The best-laid plans and all that. He should have had plenty of time to escape before the yacht sank, but the excitement, or the exertion involved in holding the yacht, must have brought on the heart attack.' She wept quietly for a moment then pressed on, determined to say it all. 'He must have felt the attack coming on as he was boring the third hole. I imagine he reached for his tablets which he always kept in his breast pocket, undid the cap, took a tablet perhaps, but was overwhelmed as the water rushed in.'

'I can't believe it,' said Shelley. 'Why did he go to so much trouble? You were comfortably off.'

'Karel knew that his weak heart would stop him working before long. He decided to make a killing, as he put it. He would hide the diamonds for at least a year then hand in his notice, due to ill health. We would move to the Caribbean and live a life of luxury for the rest of our days. The dreams he had! Running away like that wasn't my idea of living, but I went along with it because he was so determined and because...I loved him.'

'What did you do after you realised Karel had perished?' asked Frank. 'My God! You had the diamonds! You must have known the house would be searched.'

'Yes. But at that stage I didn't know Karel was dead. I knew something had gone wrong and my only thought was to hide the diamonds.' She permitted herself a little smile. 'I simply went into Zandvoort on the bus and deposited the sealed box in a left luggage locker at the station. I added the key to my key-ring and returned home.'

'Ingenious,' said Frank dryly. 'You were taking a terrific risk. Didn't the police ask about the key?'

'They didn't notice it. By the time they arrived I was in a terrible state—as a bereaved woman is expected to be. They were local men, known to me personally, and they didn't really believe I was involved. That was my strength. They searched the house and garden, but only glanced in my purse. Any moment I expected to be found out, but I wasn't. When the fuss died down I started work on the bust of Karel. It was the perfect hiding place for the diamonds.' She smoothed her hair with nervous fingers. 'So you see why I didn't want the yacht found. Karel chose a stretch of water that was deep and murky. He knew the insurance company would try to find the yacht but expected them to draw a blank. In the event of them being successful however, he was prepared for us to leave the country at a moment's notice—with his precious haul. Well, they did draw a blank and I thought the matter was over.' She shrugged helplessly. 'When Joustra arrived I knew of his reputation and was worried. He was the one person who might be able to find the yacht. If the police saw the holes and the empty water-tight compartment, I knew it wouldn't take them long to work out what had happened.' She stared at Frank. 'I'm sorry. I tried to make amends by inviting Shelley to live here. Not that I haven't enjoyed her company...'

Frank scratched his head. 'Why, Lorraine? Why did Karel take the *Angela Rose?*'

She spoke directly to him, as if they were alone in the room. 'To discredit you, kill two birds—get the diamonds and send you to Carey Street. He never said as much but he'd been jealous of you all these years, because you and I were lovers before he met me. After Angela died he accused me of cheating with you behind his back. I could never make him believe it was all in his mind. I felt so sorry for him. It's the reason I went along with his scheme. And why I've said nothing till now, even though it meant hurting you.' She sighed deeply. 'I don't regret helping Karel. My one regret is deceiving you, seeing you suffer, discredited, your business in ruins.'

Shelley was shaken by all these revelations. Parents weren't supposed to have weaknesses and secrets...

Lorraine's trial, three months later, was front page news. It had everything—a beautiful ex-model defendant, a fortune in diamonds, a mystery death at sea, the bankruptcy of an inventor.

The charges were conspiracy to steal and being in possession of stolen property.

She was fortunate in having the sympathetic *Mijnheer* Heusden to judge her case. He declared she had been a victim of Karel's avarice and recommended mercy.

The verdict came a week later. Lorraine

was found guilty on both counts, given a suspended sentence of two years and ordered to pay costs. She was plainly relieved.

Poor Lorraine, thought Shelley, branded a liar and a thief. What men did to women! What women did for love!

It was all that Dutchman's fault. Everything that had happened, including her own bitter experiences, had stemmed from Karel's greed.

CHAPTER 10

Dirk had been called to give evidence at the trial and had taken a room at the Hotel Klokken for the duration.

It was inevitable he and Shelley would meet sooner or later. It turned out to be later, on the day after the trial ended, in fact.

Thinking the dining-room was empty, Shelley went to clear the breakfast tables and her heart accelerated at the sight of him, in a cashmere sweater the exact cornflower blue of his eyes, sitting at a table draining a cup of coffee.

She stood in the doorway, her legs seemingly paralysed, gazing at the back of his blond head for a long time. Then summoning her strength, she walked briskly into the room and banged the tray down on the sideboard.

The sound made him turn. 'That's that then,' he addressed her as she noisily gathered the plates from a neighbouring table. 'The trial is over and Lorraine van Hoorn comes out of it smelling of roses. Wouldn't you just know it?'

'I expect the judge thought she'd suffered enough,' Shelley replied. 'It's true. She was out of her mind with worry.'

'I'll bet!' He laughed shortly. 'Worried she might be found out.'

She glared at him. 'Lorraine has been like a mother to me and I know her. Stealing is out of character for her. She's basically an honest person.'

'There's that old loyalty again.' His tone contained a grudging admiration.

'She was under Karel's spell,' Shelley persisted. 'She loved him but he was a jealous man. She felt guilty because...because she could never quite convince him of her love. It's the only explanation I can see for her behaviour.'

'Love and guilt and jealousy,' Dirk mused, dabbing his mouth with the table napkin and throwing it down. 'The strongest emotions in the human character.'

She picked up the cutlery, but her hands were trembling and she dropped them on to the floor with a clatter, cursing herself for letting him see how affected she was by his nearness.

His eyes missed nothing. 'Am I bothering you?'

She bent to retrieve knives and forks. 'Huh!'

'Is that yes or no?'

Straightening, she hissed, 'Shut up you...you two-timing cheat!' She regretted her outburst immediately. She wanted him to think she had forgotten about him and the humiliation he had caused her. Now he would know his betrayal still rankled.

'I thought I'd explained all that,' he replied impatiently.

'Not to my satisfaction.'

'Okay, okay. Let's drop the subject.' He rose and took a herringbone-tweed jacket from the back of the chair. 'I must be on my way. This trial has taken up enough of my time.'

A pang of misery stabbed her, deep inside. He was leaving. She really would have no cause to see him again.

'By the way.' He shrugged the jacket on. 'The insurance company aren't paying the fifty per cent for the diamonds. It wasn't my salvage which unearthed them, so the contract's void.'

'Oh, I'm sorry, after you put in so much effort too. It's because of you my father's reputation is restored.' She would always be grateful to him for that.

He grinned slyly. 'All is not lost. There's a five per cent reward for their recovery.' He paused dramatically, eyeing her up and down. 'They're giving fifty per cent of that to each of us—you and me.'

There was a long silence while she allowed his words to sink in. 'Sorry?'

'I suggested where to look for the gems but I couldn't have carried out the search without you.'

She did a rapid calculation. Fifty per cent of five per cent of a million pounds. 'Twenty-five thousand pounds? Is that what I'll get?' her eyes grew wide. 'That's wonderful. I'll be able to help Daddy get started again.'

'You're a funny girl.' He chuckled. 'A windfall like that and all you can think of is dear old dad.'

She regarded him suspiciously. 'Did you have anything to do with my getting half of the reward? You're not trying to patronise me, are you...?'

He laughed harshly. 'Darling, lovely as you are, even your favours aren't worth twenty-five thousand pounds!'

She winced, knowing she'd asked for that.

'Thank you.' Her eyes flashed mutinously. 'That sounds like a marvellous exit line. Hadn't you better go?'

'Consider it done!'

She watched him walk away between the tables.

At the door he turned. 'It would never have worked out, you know. Us. You're too suspicious of people. You want to try trusting a little more.'

'I've tried trusting people!' she burst out. 'They have a habit of letting me down.'

'A lot of it's in your own mind...'

'Oh...get out!'

'You can make a career out of hating

188

me, you know.' With that he swivelled on his heel and was gone.

For agonising moments she stood there wanting to call him back, thinking of all the things she should have said. Anything to stop him walking out of her life for ever. But an image flashed before her eyes, of Greet, her hair gloriously fanned out over the pillows of his bed, and she bit back the inclination. Let him go! It was best this way. Dirk Joustra was not the man for her. He didn't love her. She would get over him in time. She had to.

That evening she was doing her stint at the reception desk, writing in the bookings for the next day, when the phone at her elbow rang.

It was Ryder calling from Friesland and asking to speak to Dirk.

'He left, this morning.'

'Is that you, Shelley?' Ryder was bubbling with excitement. 'Guess what?'

She was in low spirits and didn't want to be reminded of past loves. 'I'm not in the mood for guessing games.'

'I'll just have to tell you then. I'm going to be a father!'

To her surprise she felt genuinely

happy for him. 'That's wonderful. Congratulations!'

'Yeah, some time in the spring, the doc says.'

'How's Tilda?'

'Her general health is good but I'll be taking extra care of her over the next few months. She wants to carry on with the boutique for as long as she is able, then we'll get a manageress in...'

As she listened to his laugh-filled voice she realised she didn't hate him any longer. He was a good man. He had come along when she needed a shoulder to lean on. He had loved her at first but his love had been the fleeting kind. He hadn't wanted to hurt her, but what else could he do? Faced with his honesty she'd been unable to cope. After being so dependent on him she had allowed the shock of his leaving to cloud all the happiness and peace of mind he had brought her.

'Ryder.'

'Yes, dear?'

'I'm sorry...for the way I behaved...the things I said. You were right and I was wrong. I know that now. Tilda's a lucky girl and I wish you both all the happiness...'

She was too choked to continue.

'Thank you, dear. You're going to be okay.'

She handed over the desk to old Popken and went outside. The air struck cold and she wrapped her jacket tighter around her. It would soon be December and the nights were already drawing in. The new moon was rising high, a silver crescent standing on end. She contemplated it, thinking of that other, bad moon which had heralded the stormy days ahead. Past history! She was a survivor. She had proved it.

Now she was ready for the next chapter in her life.

The cheque arrived a couple of weeks later and Shelley handed it to her father. He hadn't wanted to take it at first but she insisted, so it had been agreed they would form a partnership and start a new boatyard here in Holland.

He smiled affectionately. 'Twenty-five thousand pounds will just about pay off the creditors. And as a discharged bankrupt I'll be able to take out a loan. That and what I earned in Saudi Arabia should be enough to start a small yard with some living accommodation attached. If you like, you can work as the firm's secretary, as you did in Tilbury.'

'Sounds great!'

He stared round at the comfortable kitchen with its Delft tiling and traditional stove. 'It's been nice staying here with Lorraine but we can't encroach on her generosity any longer. She wants to sell the bungalow to pay the court costs. Perhaps when we're settled she could come and live with us. She'll be lonely after we've left, especially now that Greet's gone back to the south of France.' He chuckled. 'To look for a millionaire!'

'You still think a lot of Lorraine, don't you?'

'Yes.' A far-away look filled his eyes. 'Nothing's changed between us.'

Shelley grinned.

'I know what you're thinking. No fool like an old fool.'

'On the contrary, I think it's wonderful.'

The next few weeks were hectic and exciting for the Pearsons. Frank took a lease on a run-down boatyard ten miles away, at Spaaerndam, the celebrated village where long ago, according to legend, a boy called Pieter had put his thumb in a hole in the dyke and prevented a national catastrophe.

It was a pretty area. The yard was next to the canal and a tumbledown house went with the lease. The building needed money spending on it—something they didn't have but they worked hard to make a few rooms habitable, including an office in the corner of the workshop for Shelley.

Frank's fine reputation as a boatbuilder was unimpaired, especially now he had been exonerated from any involvement with the sinking of the *Angela Rose,* and as soon as word of the new yard circulated the orders started to come in. He bought a second-hand van and talked about taking on an apprentice.

'Things are looking up,' said Shelley. 'And I know you're going to make it this time, without Karel van Hoorn standing by to shove a spanner in the works. Why, before you know it you'll be in the buoyancy tank business again.'

Frank's expression was wistful. 'No, that's all in the past. If I think along those lines I'll only be fooling myself.'

She gave him a hug. 'I'm not so sure. I have great faith in you.'

He grinned. 'Thanks for that vote of confidence.'

Shelley shivered as she crossed the chilly workshop, picking her way between drawing-boards, charts, wood shavings and sheets of fibre glass. February had been cold and wet with an ethereal mist hanging over the canal most days.

Scooping up the mail from the mat she went into her office where the stove still held yesterday's ashes. She raked it and laid more logs and soon had a bright blaze going.

The room was small with just enough room for the desk and a couple of filing cabinets. There wasn't much for her to do and she was aware her job could be carried out by a part-time clerk, but it was pleasant working with her father again and she had time now to cook nourishing meals for him.

She was slitting open the envelopes when Frank, in spotless white overalls, popped his head round the door. 'I've got an important visitor coming this morning so we must make a bit of a fuss over him. He might put some money in the business.'

'Hey, what's all this?' she asked, jumping

up and grabbing a duster. 'Why didn't you tell me you had a backer? I thought I was a partner in this 'ere firm.'

'Sorry, love, I was going to. I met him in a bar last night and haven't had the chance. The minute he arrives I'll pop indoors to wash and put on a suit while you entertain him.'

'Rightio. We could do with a backer.' She tapped the pile of bills she had taken from their envelopes. 'The wolf is knocking at the door.'

She tidied and dusted the office and cleaned the window. An hour later she was typing an order list when she heard voices outside.

Frank opened the office door and whispered urgently, 'He's here. I'll just go and change. Make him a cup of coffee.'

The man, dressed in a sheepskin jacket, had his back to her. Very tall, very lean, very blond. She thought she felt the earth move and gave herself a mental ticking off for letting her senses play tricks on her. With a shiver that had nothing to do with the weather she went outside.

'Shelley.' Dirk turned his brilliant blue eyes on her. 'It's good to see you again.'

She grabbed the work-bench, waiting for

the world to steady and her heartbeat to return to normal.

His eyes travelled over her red angora sweater, the wide belt emphasising her small waist, her Royal Stewart tartan slacks and black ankle boots. 'You've lost weight, which you can't afford to do.'

'Yes, I suppose I have.' Misery affected her that way. 'You look well.'

'It's the outdoor life.'

'Coffee?' She dragged her wobbly legs back into the office.

'Please.' He perched on the desk while she operated the percolator.

Her hands shook and more coffee went on the table than in the jug. 'So you're the mysterious backer.'

'Yes.' He swung his leg idly. 'Frank tells me you've put your share of the reward into the firm and I want to do the same.'

'Sorry?'

'You heard me.'

She surveyed him steadily. 'But why? You know nothing about us.'

'That's where you're wrong. I know a great deal about you. I know you're loyal and have integrity. What better credentials?'

'Charity, then?' Her eyes fiercely opposed his. 'We don't want your money...'

'Now don't go jumping to conclusions. Remember *trompe-l'oeil*. I don't put my money into worthless schemes. I shall expect a fair return for my investment. Frank is wasted on boatbuilding. The buoyancy tank idea was a good one and he deserves the chance to develop it. It's a business deal, pure and simple.'

Suddenly that wasn't the answer she wanted.

She busied herself with the coffee. As she handed him an earthenware mug their fingers touched. She jumped as if she'd glanced a hot stove.

He took a sip then looked round, spotting the little toy panda nestling among the invoices on the cabinet. 'That looks familiar. I do believe I won it at the *Kermis*. I wonder why you kept it.'

She drew a rasping breath. She had kept everything he had given her, the water pistol, the china dog, even the coconut. And she had pressed one of the hyacinths he had bought her that day in the bulbfields. But she wasn't going to tell him that.

'You're wrong. I bought it in Zandvoort.'

His eyes called her a liar.

She looked towards the door. Her father was taking a long time to change. And why did he want to change anyway? There was nothing wrong with overalls. He was a working man...

As Dirk followed her gaze she wondered if this had all been set up and the colour rushed to her cheeks. 'Oh I get it.' She was angry now, out of her depth, and wanting to strike back. 'Well, if you think you're going to walk in here and make grandiose gestures with your money and expect me to fall at your feet, you're very much mistaken.'

He set the mug down and straightened from the desk, his face a bitter mask. 'I'm wasting my time here. I might as well go.'

A great tremor snaked through her.

She took herself in hand. What were her feelings for this man? Her desire for him was basic yet emotive and she detected a king-sized hunger in him that she wanted to assuage, then rekindle, then assuage again. Her need both thrilled and weakened her in a way she had known only once before, in his bedroom in Friesland.

His very presence warmed her blood and set every nerve a-jangle, but above all was an inborn admiration for the power in him, the energy, the red-bloodedness—which she could equal! He had explained about Greet and she wanted to believe him. *Would* believe him. It was time to start trusting again. She must make her feelings known, take a hand in the forging of her own destiny—no matter what it cost her in pride.

She said clearly, 'Don't go.'

'Why not?'

She gulped. She was in it now, up to her neck, and might as well venture on to the end. 'Because...I love you.'

'That's all I wanted to know.' His hands came to rest on her shoulders and she leaned against him, conscious of his strength, tempered with gentleness, which she knew instinctively could be relied upon.

A tidal wave of euphoria broke over her and she wallowed in it.

'Dearest Shelley!' He imprisoned her in his sheep-skinned arms and rubbed his smooth chin against her temple. 'I've thought of no-one but you since the day we met. *Ik houd van jou.* I love you.' His kiss was hard and demanding and it made her dizzy.

'I never intended falling in love with you.' His words vibrated against her throat. 'I just wanted to keep you away from Ryder. You were right about that. At least I thought that was my motive. But somewhere along the way love happened. Don't ask me when.' His fingers sifted through her long hair. 'I've been pretty mixed up.'

She hugged him tightly. 'Welcome to the club.'

The coffee grew cold while he kissed her. There could have been an earthquake for all either of them knew, so lost were they in their benediction of love.

'Before we go any further,' he murmured as he paused for breath, 'I'd like to clear up any misunderstandings you may have about Greet...'

'No need...'

'No, I want to. She offered herself to me but nothing happened. I escorted her about for company, more than anything.'

'I know. Poor Greet!'

'Poor Greet, be blowed!'

They smiled crazily at each other.

He stroked her cheek. 'We have plans

to make. I want you so much.'

She trembled afresh. What had he in mind? Marriage—or an affair? She thought she knew the answer. Why should he want to marry her? She wasn't Friesian. She wasn't even Dutch. And she certainly wasn't blonde! She could mess up that pure strain... An affair was not ideally what she wanted, but it was what she would settle for. Yes, it would be an affair...

'Marry me, Shelley!'

Her spirit burst free, like a lark taking to the heavens. She laughed out loud. 'Oh Dirk, yes, yes, yes! I was so frightened you weren't going to ask me.'

'Don't you see?' he whispered urgently. 'I have to marry you. I have to shackle you to me, till death us do part. I can't live without you. Believe me, I've tried.' He buried his lips in her hair and his voice was muffled. *Lieveling*. It's been hell without you. I'll love you always and never be untrue.'

'Hm! Me too!'

'Let's go and buy an engagement ring. Sapphires, I think, to match your eyes.' He grinned wryly. 'Not diamonds!'

Someone coughed nearby and she saw

her father, still in his overalls, proving her earlier supposition to be correct.

'Everything all right?' he asked, looking from one to the other of their radiant faces. 'Are congratulations in order?'

'I'll say!' said Dirk.

The two men shook hands and Frank kissed his daughter's flushed cheeks. 'I suppose you'll be taking her away to Friesland?'

'Yes,' said Dirk. Then, 'If that suits you, *lieveling*. I mean, we can live anywhere...'

'It suits me fine. Daddy can manage without me. But I shall want to work. That is, until...' Her blush deepened.

'The children come along!' Dirk squeezed her hand and she felt goose-pimples galloping up her arm. 'You can be my secretary if you wish, look after my office and accompany me abroad from time to time. Or start your own business, the same as Tilda has done...'

'We'll see.'

'And we'll keep in touch with Pearson Marine,' he assured her father. 'We both have a vested interest in it after all.'

'Well, I'll be sorry to lose her,' said Frank.

Shelley said, 'Perhaps Lorraine will help

you out with the office work.'

'Perhaps she will.' They exchanged a grin.

Frank went back towards the house, calling over his shoulder, 'Come indoors, both of you. I'll find a bottle of something so we can drink to the happy news.'

Dirk picked up Shelley's cardigan from the back of the chair and draped it round her shoulders. Bringing his chin to rest against her temple he murmured, 'How about an Easter wedding?'

'What's the rush?'

'I want you so much. Not just physically— though the Lord knows I do—but spiritually too. An early marriage makes sense.'

A delicious tingle zigzagged down her spine. 'Yes indeed.'

He kissed the tip of her nose.

'It's not true then,' she reflected.

'What isn't?'

'That quotation about the Dutch giving too little and taking too much. You've given me everything.'

'I shall continue to do so.' His cornflower eyes brimmed with adoration. 'If you're not happy then it won't be this Dutchman's fault!'

The publishers hope that this book has given you enjoyable reading. Large Print Books are especially designed to be as easy to see and hold as possible. If you wish a complete list of our books, please ask at your local library or write directly to: Dales Large Print Books, Long Preston, North Yorkshire, BD23 4ND, England.

This Large Print Book for the Partially sighted, who cannot read normal print, is published under the auspices of

THE ULVERSCROFT FOUNDATION

THE ULVERSCROFT FOUNDATION

. . . we hope that you have enjoyed this Large Print Book. Please think for a moment about those people who have worse eyesight problems than you . . . and are unable to even read or enjoy Large Print, without great difficulty.

You can help them by sending a donation, large or small to:

**The Ulverscroft Foundation,
1, The Green, Bradgate Road,
Anstey, Leicestershire, LE7 7FU,
England.**
or request a copy of our brochure for more details.

The Foundation will use all your help to assist those people who are handicapped by various sight problems and need special attention.

Thank you very much for your help.